CYRIEL BUYSSE

THE AUNTS

TRANSLATED BY DAVID MCKAY

THIS IS A SNUGGLY BOOK

ISBN: 978-1-64525-054-8

This book was published with the support of
Flanders Literature (flandersliterature.be).

THE AUNTS

CYRIEL BUYSSE (1859–1932) was expected to follow in his father's footsteps as director of a chicory factory, but under the influence of his aunt, the well-known writer Virginie Loveling, he instead became a novelist and playwright, one of the great storytellers of the Dutch-speaking world. His early work, influenced by French naturalism, was bleak in mood, depicting the miserable lives of the rural poor in what was still practically a feudal society. His later work has a lighter touch and expresses his ironic humor, psychological insight, and love of the Flemish landscape. His novels written after World War I, such as *The Aunts*, reflect the dawning of a modern sensibility in Flanders, and their spare prose sometimes gives them a remarkably contemporary feel.

DAVID MCKAY is an award-winning literary translator who lives in The Hague. His recent publications include *Adrift in the Middle Kingdom* by J. Slauerhoff, a poetic adventure novel in a China on the brink of revolution which gradually transforms into a surreal fantasy, and Multatuli's classic political novel *Max Havelaar* about Dutch misrule in the East Indies, a joint translation with Ina Rilke that was shortlisted for the Oxford Weidenfeld Prize.

CONTENTS

TRANSLATOR'S NOTE

THIS novella is set in and around an unnamed rural village in the province of East Flanders, Belgium, around 1920. At the time of the story, the Flemish upper and middle classes were generally bilingual, and French was the main language of government and elite communications, while the working classes spoke Dutch. Furthermore, Flemish speakers of Dutch used (and still use) many French words and phrases, in every segment of society. The characters in this story tend to speak Dutch peppered with French; certain uses of French are typical of particular characters. All in all, the use of French plays a significant role in Buysse's narrative and characterization. For that reason, I have left a good deal of French in this translation. French phrases and sentences that may be unclear are translated in footnotes.

In addition to using French, the characters also switch back and forth between standard Dutch and the local Dutch dialect. Standard Dutch is generally used by the narrator and by middle and upper-class characters speaking to one another, whereas East Flemish dialect is used by and with working-class characters. The fictional variety of English employed here to render East Flemish dialect is inspired in large part by the colloquial speech of Derbyshire and other regions of northern England, as presented in the novels of D.H. Lawrence and elsewhere. Considering the social, economic, and cultural similarities between Lawrence's northern England and Buysse's Flanders, as well as the similar themes addressed by the two authors, I felt justified in invoking the spirit of Lawrence here.

I am once again grateful to David Colmer for his insightful comments. F. Philip Holland's *Words of the White Peak* was one valuable resource for rendering East Flemish dialect into English. Many thanks also to the publisher, Snuggly Books, for taking an interest in this lesser-known classic. Although it is not my role to thank Flanders Literature for their financial support to the publisher, I do thank them wholeheartedly for the support and appreciation they have always shown to translators, their hospitality to visiting translators in Antwerp, and the dedication with which they promote great Flemish writing.

—David McKay

THE AUNTS

I.

THE wedding dinner was drawing to a close. A few men had already lit their cigarettes, and the weightless blue smoke curled past their reddened faces, sometimes lingering around the women's hair like a filmy veil.

The hazy gray light of the November day was slowly fading, and the far corners of the large dining room were filling with shadow. The young newlyweds, who stood side by side with their backs to one of the windows, were becoming dark silhouettes outlined against the bright pane.

Dessert was finished; the glasses remained half-drunk and were no longer emptied or refilled. They were all growing tired, all sated. A few conversations were still lively and animated, but most of the guests sat stiff and silent, waiting to see who would give the signal to leave the stuffy room.

Marie slowly rose to her feet, and right away Max followed suit. Sudden silence fell over the long tables. They quietly threaded their way around the chairs to where Mr. Dufour was seated. Max leaned in to whisper.

"Papa, time for us to go."

Mr. Dufour, still engrossed in conversation with the woman next to him, looked up in surprise.

"Already!"

"Yes, Papa, it's four o'clock and the carriage is waiting," Marie replied.

Mr. Dufour stood, and this was a sign for everyone to stand; in a flurry of discarded napkins and shifted chairs, they prepared to say farewell to the bride and groom.

"Well then, *bon voyage!*" said Mr. Dufour, and his voice, though as gruff as ever, betrayed a quiver of emotion.

He reached out his arms and embraced first his son and then his daughter-in-law. His eyes were wet, and his lower lip was pursed tight beneath his bristly mustache. He could not recall having put his arms around any of his children in years.

"*Bon voyage!* . . . and a safe homecoming!" he repeated, with a slight catch in his voice. His hands trembled slightly.

"You go ahead and sit down again, Papa. Stay with your guests," Max said sedately.

Mr. Dufour, stifling his emotion, obeyed without protest.

The young couple shuffled down the long row of chairs. Max was smiling. His triumphant eyes beamed with happiness, lighting up his regular features and full, dark beard. His whole being glowed with self-confident strength, as if entrusted with a treasure he meant to defend with all his might. Marie, beside him, moved through the room with a silent modesty, a kind of submissiveness. The guests sensed that she had bid all independence a final farewell. She looked very slender, even a little gaunt, in her long, white wedding dress embellished with orange blossom. Her delicate veil, tucked back over her shoulders, formed a sweet, mild, decorative frame around the perfect oval of her face, her dark hair, and her dark, mild eyes. She was not what is called pretty, but she was graceful.

She reached the Aunts. There were three Aunts, Mr. Dufour's sisters: Aunt Clemence, Aunt Estelle, and Aunt Victoire. Aunt Clemence's gentle name was undeserved. She had a hard, tight face with sharp features, the female counterpart of her brother's. That hardness was not in any way tempered by her straight, blonde hair, nor by her light blue eyes, as cold as steel and usually full of stern disapproval.

Aunt Estelle, in contrast, appeared—and was—the very model of goodness and gentleness.

Her smile was always so friendly, and her hair, which at an early age had gone a silvery gray, reinforced the impression that this was a good-natured woman, affectionate, amiable, and mild. Was that her nature? Or was it her tragic love affair, which had left her whole life a colorless wreck?

For a while, these three sisters had been at war with one another. The eldest, a bitter man-hater, as well as the youngest, who had never received so much as a glance from any man, had categorically disapproved of Estelle's choice and would not be reconciled with her until she had given up her marriage plans once and for all.

Then Aunt Estelle had fallen ill, and ever since she'd been weak, without any will of her own, completely under the thumb of her older, stronger sister. She was often even ordered about by her difficult younger sibling, Aunt Victoire. Even though Victoire was the youngest, she looked like the eldest of the three. She had a pale, ugly face with wrinkles along her nose and bags under her peevish eyes; and her large mouth full of false teeth always seemed to be grumbling and huffing behind tight-shut lips, as if frothing with the never-ending rage and resentment that nature had bestowed her with so little grace. Disliking young people and amusement, she sought her consolation in the church, where she and her sisters were among the most faithful members of the flock.

"Aunt Clemence—" Max began, making a deep bow to the old spinster before departing. When he faced the Aunts—who were certain never to marry, and whose entire fortune he and sisters expected to inherit—all his robust self-confidence fell away. As always, he felt, in their presence, as if he were still a very small boy. He would never have taken Marie as his bride if the choice had in any way offended the Aunts' sensibilities. Fortunately, they had all shown mercy on him and given their blessing, and yet . . . to them, his marriage seemed something like an unexpected extravagance of his, which they could agree to overlook as long as it remained wholly virtuous and respectable and *comme il faut*, without a single stain or blot.

"Max . . ." Aunt Clemence responded, looking her nephew straight in the eyes as she held out her hand. "Will you take every sort of care, Max . . . and see to it that your marriage is never anything but a comfort, an honor, and a pleasure to us?"

Even though Max was uncertain exactly what Aunt Clemence meant by this, he was quick to say yes, shaking her hand with vigor as if sealing a solemn promise with a vow.

"And you, Marie? Can I expect the same of you?" Clemence repeated, now fixing her eyes on the bride.

"Oh, yes, Aunt! Oh, yes!" Marie confirmed in a shaky voice. Her cheeks were suddenly burning under the thin bridal veil; she had lost all sense of what to do or say. A feeling of guilt overwhelmed her as she stood in her wedding dress before that hard, tight-faced spinster, and in her bewilderment she leaned forward and gave her a soft, trembling kiss on one cheek, then the other.

It was like kissing leather. At first, Aunt Clemence seemed about to draw back, but instead she let it happen. She did not, however, kiss Marie in return.

After that, saying goodbye to kindly Aunt Estelle was like a soothing balm to Marie's soul. Estelle, of course, was nothing but good and kind, and her warm wishes for them could not have been more heartfelt. Aunt Victoire, on the other hand, was far from friendly or approachable. One of her dark moods had come over her, and averting her eyes, she abruptly asked the newlyweds, "You do realize marriage is a very serious business?"

"Why yes, Aunt! Of course, Aunt!" they cringed.

"You know it's no foolish farce, no laughing matter?" Aunt Victoire continued spitefully. And she gave another internal huff behind tight, scowling lips.

"Of course, Aunt, of course."

"I hope your marriage will be a *fine* thing, a *pure* thing, and not some foolish farce."

"It will be, Aunt, we promise."

Disconcerted, Max shook her hand and Marie kissed her on the cheeks as she had Aunt Clemence and Aunt Estelle. And like Aunt Clemence, Aunt Victoire let herself be kissed but did not kiss back. All she did was make a strange, internal noise in her closed mouth.

The young couple, now in a hurry, went from table to table shaking hands. Max exchanged a quick double handshake with his bosom friend Raymond, and last of all they came to Clara, Adrienne, and Edmée, Max's three sisters, who accompanied them to the front door.

All three of the young women had tears in their eyes. They were laughing and crying at once. They were happy, and they were sad. That was to be expected, under the circumstances. Unlike their father and the Aunts, they pictured themselves in Marie's place. They had grown to appreciate her during the few months of the engagement. And they also felt a tender pity for her, because she had never known her parents, who had both died when she was small, one soon after the other. She had spent her childhood and youth in the care of an old, ailing aunt, who by the time of the wedding had not left her bed in years. That was why the ceremony had taken place, by necessity, not in the aunt's home but in Mr. Dufour's—another reason the sisters pitied Marie. Although they had lost their mother, they still had their father, at least, and a house of their own. It was their heartfelt wish and expectation that Max would always take very good care of Marie; they hoped he'd be everything to her and give her what for so many years she'd lacked: a happy home.

The time had come to part. Adrienne, the second sister, went upstairs with Marie to help her change before leaving, while Clara and Edmée returned to the dining hall.

At the insistence of Mr. Dufour, who had recovered from his brief spasm of sentiment, the guests had returned to their seats. Mr. Dufour ordered a few lamps lit, and the cluttered table soon became a festive scene again. The conversation was loud and cheerful, and the glasses were refilled. Mr. Dufour proposed that everyone remain seated for coffee and liqueur, and this prospect added to the merriment as, all around the table, cigars fumed.

Another emotional moment followed when a carriage drove up, drawn by two horses, and stopped at the open front gate. The coachman wore a top hat and had a white bow around his whip.

"They're leaving! There they go!" a voice cried. The family members and a few friends leapt to their feet and rushed to the windows. In the gathering twilight outside, they could see the suitcases being loaded. A crowd of curious onlookers had assembled in front of the houses across the street; a farmer, passing in his wagon, pulled up his horses.

Marie came through the gate and hurried toward the carriage. She turned and smiled, waving at the people in the windows. She wore a dark brown suit and a stylish black bonnet that suited her. She was no longer a girl, but a young lady. Max and Adrienne followed, Max looking very dapper in his fashionable new winter coat, Adrienne wearing a fur stole. Max, too, waved toward the windows, distinguished and self-confident, before entering the carriage. The coachman cracked his whip, and they rattled away. Glancing back through the window, they gave one final wave. They were off! The eyes of the curious crowd followed the departing vehicle.

In the dining room, the guests had returned to their seats, and Adrienne too had taken her place again, opposite Raymond, Max's dear friend. More deeply moved than her sisters, she wiped away her final tears with a sigh.

"*Partis, mademoiselle?*" Raymond asked her across the table, making polite conversation.

"*Oui*, they've left." she replied with a bashful smile, lowering her eyes.

He impressed her, as always, because of his appearance. Raymond was handsome, with dark hair, a neat mustache, and expressive eyes. It was easy to see the wolf in him, the ladies' man. In a more cosmopolitan setting, with a whiff of effeminate sophistication, he might well have seemed *too* handsome, too preening. But here, in these village circles, closer to nature, he did not go to such extremes. He had healthy good looks and a tan complexion, and there was a buoyancy in the way he moved. His smile was fresh and open, suggesting something in him that was decisive, almost daring, and yet, without a doubt, honest and good. It was pleasant to look at him. You felt drawn to him, but a trifle cautious, chiefly because of the look in his eyes—strong, sometimes almost piercing.

He lived in a place known as Carvin, half farm, half estate, just outside the village center, alone and unmarried, with his old housekeeper and his staff, and there he practiced agriculture, more as a hobby than out of any necessity. "I am a farmer, a man of the soil!" he liked to say, in a slightly affected tone, to anyone who inquired about his occupation, but his friends and acquaintances knew very well that this was more a pose than a reality, and that his farm could fairly be called an expensive pastime.

What he did most often, and most loved to do, was go out shooting and ride fine horses. To see the man as he really was, you had but to speak to him of horses and shooting parties. Then he would begin to sway in his chair as if in a saddle. His eyes would gleam, his cheeks would color, and his hands would make reining motions. Then the hours passed uncounted; he could sit all day with whoever would listen and continue the conversation.

In Max he had found a man driven by the same passions. They often went out riding and shooting together, or else they would meet to discuss their shared enthusiasms. Their bond of friendship was firm and mutual and seemed likely to last all their lives. Although Max, who was studying law, did not have nearly as much leisure time as Raymond, the hours he could spare were for his friend.

What a blow and a disappointment it was to Raymond, then, when he heard that Max was head over heels in love and intended to marry! It felt to him like a cheat, an infidelity, almost a betrayal. Above all, he resented the woman who was taking his friend away from him. Women! What place did they have in the life of a strapping young man? After all, one knew where to find them when one needed them . . . At first, Raymond teased and reproached his friend without mercy, but when he saw how very serious the question was for Max, and the deep sorrow, and eventual anger, that his gibes and reproaches provoked, he stopped and resigned himself to the inevitable with his easy and accommodating nature.

"Very well," he told Max, "marry if you must! Your marriage will mean nothing to our friendship. We can go on riding and shooting, and even visit the girls now and then, as we used to . . ."

"Not that! Never! Riding and shooting are well enough, but not the other thing, not ever again . . . Never!" Max cried with tight-lipped resolution.

"Come, come, you'll see things differently soon enough, when the novelty's faded," Raymond replied with a chuckle.

This had nearly led them to quarrel and fall out. Max had insisted he never bring up the subject again, and Raymond had thought it best to say no more about it; and now he sat meekly at his friend's wedding dinner, straight across from Max's second sister, who was sweet and warm and gentle and sometimes even pretty. Tonight, for example, she looked quite fetching in her light party dress, although Raymond was a bit disappointed by the high neckline—which perhaps was inspired by fear of the prudish, persnickety aunts. It made her look a little stiff, even now, in the commotion of the party, like a rock unmoved by crashing waves.

Raymond did not know, and had no way of knowing, Adrienne's true inner feelings toward him. He did not even suspect that she cherished any special feelings for him, because he felt nothing special for her. She was nothing more to him than his friend's very congenial sister, and it was by no means Adrienne that he saw when passion or the longing for a woman rose up in him.

If he had only known . . . known how much, and what, she felt for him! If he had only sensed, beneath the deceptive, icy crust of her reserve, the deep and silent ardor burning—so painfully sometimes! If he had only known with what feminine guile and craftiness she had arranged to be

seated opposite him at dinner! Not beside him—
that would have drawn too much attention, and
she had to preserve her secret from her sisters and
above all from Max—but opposite him, so that
she could gaze at him all afternoon, admiring him
in silence and basking in his presence.

A singular contrast! What made him so attrac-
tive to her was the very quality she lacked. She
loved his easy nature, so dashing and vigorous, his
high spirits, even when they ran away with him,
and the carefree mirth with which he went about
the world. She felt in him a kind of superiority
that she coveted and sometimes envied.

She kept all this down in her innermost depths,
never showing the slightest hint of it. Fire shot to
her cheeks whenever she thought he might notice
or sense it. She pictured the revelation of her secret
as a catastrophe that would throw her whole life
into disarray and ruin, just as a similar infatuation
had destroyed the life of her kindly Aunt Estelle.
What would her father say? What would Max
and her sisters say?! And the Aunts, the Aunts!
. . . Oddly, she did not for a moment entertain
the hypothesis that her family might welcome
the match. No, she felt strongly, intuitively, that
they would oppose it, that all of them, *all* of them
would oppose it. Why? She couldn't have said,
but she sensed it. Her feelings for Raymond were

a disaster, that much she knew, and sensing and knowing it so clearly, so deeply, she wept from time to time in sorrow and misery, yet found her passion impossible to dismiss or subdue.

Behind a soft semblance of silent contentment, Adrienne was unhappy through and through, and no one who knew her suspected it in the slightest.

Abruptly, a solemn silence fell over the merry company at the table. The Aunts were rising ceremoniously from their chairs to go. The three of them lived in a country house just outside a neighboring town, and their carriage was waiting in front of the house. They preferred to be home before utter darkness fell. With no escort but Vreesken, their old driver, they were scared to ride down the lonely, unlit roads. In a dignified row, they shuffled toward Mr. Dufour for a farewell handshake.

"*Mais non!* So soon!" he exclaimed, feigning surprise.

"It is already dark out," Aunt Clemence said, and her tight face looked almost reproachful, as if it were her brother's fault that they had stayed too long.

"It was all just lovely, just lovely!" kindly Aunt Estelle said with a smile.

What Aunt Victoire grumbled was impossible to make out, but her shriveled face had a peevish look, and behind her closed lips she appeared to be huffing.

As soon as the Aunts had risen, all three of their nieces had leapt up with them, as if on springs. Adrienne had rushed out of the room to fetch their coats, while Clara and Edmée tended to the three spinsters. It was as if their departure were an event of supreme importance, as if they were setting out on a distant and dangerous journey.

"Do take care not to catch cold, Aunt Clemence."

"Shall I turn up your fur collar, Aunt Victoire?"

They were less concerned about Aunt Estelle, who was always contented, no matter what.

As the Aunts took their leave, all the other guests, one after another, had risen to their feet. It was strange; although the elderly Aunts were anything but the life and soul of the party, their status in the Dufour family was such that it would have seemed almost indecent to go on with the festivities in their absence. One by one, all the guests came up to Mr. Dufour and his three daughters to say goodnight. Most faces shone red, and Mr. Dufour's was no exception; he was flushed with emotion and no small amount of drink. Adrienne gave Raymond a gentle smile and quickly lowered her eyes. Her hand was clammy and trembling as it pressed his. In any case, it made no impression on him. He had fallen into conversation with two of Marie's cousins, the Verstratjes—avid equestrians and hunters like himself—and was talking with them as he left, without a second glance at Adrienne. She felt a dull melancholy, which grew sharper when the last guest had left and all of a sudden the large room was empty and silent. Her father had left too, caught up in the wake, as it were, of the departing crowd. He'd needed a change of air, he'd said, and was popping out to a coffee house with a few friends; he wouldn't be long.

So there they stood, all three of them, the daughters, at loose ends, uncertain where to go or what to do with themselves. They ran their eyes over the stained tablecloths, the half-full wine glasses, and the wilting flowers, and that disorder, in all its prosaic sobriety, struck them like a blow. It was as if they happened to find themselves in some hotel or restaurant where a celebration had just ended. They no longer felt at home, especially when they noticed the unfamiliar waiters hired for the occasion, waiting stock still in the open door to clear the tables. The upstairs maid approached with a hesitant look.

※

"Miss Clara, wouldn't you like to retire to your salon while we take care of this? I'll light the lamp there for you."

"Yes, Martha, of course!" All three nodded, as if happy that someone, anyone, had come to tell them what to do next. They hurried off, and in the little salon off the large dining room, they sat by the wide window in the half-darkness and asked Martha not to light a lamp just yet, please. They would sit and chat for a while, they said, and enjoy the twilight.

A silence descended over the three of them, along with the darkness, like a thick, oppressive shroud. Only the large window still let in a grayish light from outside, and they gazed at it, motion-less, pensive, with dreaming eyes.

Where could Max and Marie be at this very moment, and what could they be doing? Now . . . now they were on the train, headed for the big city, where they would spend their wedding night together. Together . . . always together, forevermore. Together in happiness, together in sorrow, but together, always together, their whole life long. That was the beauty of marriage, the beauty of happiness. That was the purpose of life. Soon, alone in their room, far from the meaningless hubbub of humankind, he would sweep her up in a passionate embrace, kiss her, kiss her on the mouth, and say to her in a choked, shaky voice, "I am happy, Marie; I am the happiest man on earth!"

Oh, happy Marie, then, happy woman, to hear him utter those words of adoration, to be told it was she—and she alone—who made him so truly and perfectly happy! Why was that great happiness reserved for Marie and denied to each of them? What had they done . . . and what must one do to achieve it?

Bah! . . . Marie had never done a thing to deserve it, any more than the three of them had. It had settled upon her unbidden, as the silent dew of night settles on the plants; it had smiled at her and brushed up against her; all she'd had to do was return the smile and say yes.

They sat pondering and staring, three vague silhouettes in useless party clothes by the wide window, against the gray twilight outside. From the large dining room, they heard muffled sounds of the tables being cleared; the slight clink of crystal or silver, one plate tapping another, a faint buzz of voices—the last dying reverberations of joy and merriment. It was over now and would never return. Even if the tables were laid again one day for a similar occasion, it would be quite different. A moment gone by would never, ever return.

There was a soft knock at the door. All three were startled out of their musings, and Clara said:

"You may enter."

"*Pardon, mademoiselle*," said Martha, entering quietly, "does ye know if yer Papa will be 'ome for supper?"

Supper? They hadn't given it a moment's thought; none of them wished to eat anything more. No, supper was out of the question.

The maid withdrew as quietly as she had entered, but her spectral appearance had broken the mood, and as they awoke from their formless, wistful reverie, they were conscious again of the dry, commonplace reality that surrounded them and had made up their world for as long as they could remember.

They felt a piercing ache at the hopeless solitude and desolation of their lives. They hated the village where they lived, where they had to live; they hated it because it was killing them. They had no one there to keep them company; there were no young ladies of their age and class; there were no young people with whom they could let down their guard; there was nothing, no one; they were buried alive, body and soul smothered. The village—that was the long street of narrow, tight-shut houses, which seemed to conceal dour reclusiveness or small-minded envy; the village was the brewer, the distiller, the coal merchant, and other worthies, including her father, all tippling at preordained hours in musty taverns; the village was the weekly procession of farm families bringing their animals and other produce to the market square; and beyond that, the village was death, the grave, the sorrow and tedium of every moment. Their sole consolation and refuge was the church, which they visited twice a day, morning and evening, as loyal and punctual as the tippling worthies at the local taverns.

There, in the church, the soul was purified and the whole being exalted. Each visit was an hour passed outside their circumscribed sphere, in a kind of intoxicating, mystic, sensual ecstasy. The church was for the women; there they felt at home, there they lived their own, deepest lives. They felt a close bond with the other women who kneeled there in the dim, incense-scented atmosphere; they became nuns of a sort, and their rapturous souls full of mystical longings seemed to merge with the souls of the dear little sisters from the convent, who were always, *always* there too, sunk so deep in silent devotion that they looked like nothing more than immaterial figures, motionless, hieratic apparitions, like the ones in the high stained-glass windows. And the priest and his assistants, too, seemed cleansed and spiritualized, and in their long, flowing robes, with their solemn songs and soothing gestures, they too were no longer solid creatures, but exalted beings of faith and goodness, in harmony with the mood among the women.

Such was the everyday poetry that made life bearable, that never failed to bring sweet comfort and consolation to the coarse and sobering reality of their lives.

Twilight had given way to night now. The large window was black against the blackness of the street, where only a few feeble lights glowed sadly in the houses across the way, and still the three sisters remained in motionless reverie, with no more than a word now and then, their eyes staring through the darkness at the wistful scenes conjured up by their stifled spirits. What were they to do with themselves?! What was to become of them? Would they gradually resign themselves to the fate of their three maiden Aunts, or would someone come at last to lead them into life in all its beauty, as Max had come for Marie? They had not yet given up all hope, but they were so full of fear. They sensed so many obstacles around them; they saw so little light in the distance. It should have arrived by now; they'd been waiting so long. Clara was thirty, Adrienne twenty-eight, Edmée twenty-five. Sometimes they felt old already; they were starting to resemble their elderly Aunts. Clara was much like Aunt Clemence and looked more like her every day; Adrienne was reminiscent of kindly Aunt Estelle. Only Edmée was not like any of them, but her health was poor and she seemed only half alive; her weak eyes and unfortunate complexion always gave her face a pale, sleepy look, as if she had never entirely woken up.

The idea . . . the idea that they would one day turn, one day wither, into the three older Aunts, was the fear and horror that ran through their whole existence. Within themselves, they fought against that specter, but without ever finding the strength to escape the murderous oppression. The crux of the matter was that the three old Aunts, although no one ever said it in so many words, secretly wielded absolute power over the lives and futures of their three nieces. They were wealthy, and their fortune was destined to enrich their nieces one day. That fortune was the heart of the matter; because of that fortune, the three young women could never permit themselves any action that might incur the Aunts' disapproval or offend them. Max could never have married Marie if the Aunts had not finally consented to the match; how much more unthinkable for the nieces to marry without the Aunts' approval. That was the way things were, the great law underlying the lives of the Dufour family, and it could never change. The Aunts reigned supreme!

The salon door opened, and the glaring lamp-light from the corridor fell on the heavy features of Mr. Dufour.

"What!? Still in darkness?" he exclaimed in surprise. "Have you had your supper?"

"None of us were hungry," Clara said in a flat tone.

Mr. Dufour let out a buttery, well-fed laugh.

"*Le diner était bon*, eh?"

"*Très bon*," they replied calmly.

"*Enfin, c'était une belle journée*, a beautiful day!" boasted Mr. Dufour, with conviction.

"A beautiful day . . ." they echoed.

"*Max a fait un bon choix, un excellent choix!*" Mr. Dufour went on in excitement. "*Une belle fortune, une jolie fille, et des espérances! des espérances!*"[1]

The girls said nothing more. They too had *espérances*; if only they had the solid realities to

_____

1 Max has made a good choice, an excellent choice! A fine fortune, a pretty girl, and high hopes! High hopes!

match! Their father's eager enthusiasm irritated them a little, especially Clara, who could sometimes lash out unexpectedly. Despite her best efforts, she could not keep her bitter thoughts to herself.

"I hope that one day we may be so fortunate."

Mr. Dufour's hand swished through the darkness in surprise, as if to ward something off.

"Time aplenty for you; time aplenty!" he protested.

"Oh, yes," Clara snarled, "there is always plenty of time for us! Another year or two—what difference does it make? But do not forget: I am past thirty, and Adrienne is twenty-eight, and Edmée will soon be twenty-six, while Marie has not yet turned twenty-three."

"*Qu'est-ce ça prouve?!* What does that prove?!" Mr. Dufour repeated, with a casual, harried shrug of the shoulders.

"There is nothing here for us, nothing, nothing!" Clara snapped. And at that, she burst into tears.

Mr. Dufour, Adrienne, and Edmée all winced in shock.

" Come now . . . come now . . ." said Mr. Dufour, trying to appease her. "*Du calme, du calme, les servantes pourraient nous entendre.*"[1]

---

1 Calm down, calm down, the servants could hear us.

"Let us light a lamp," Adrienne suggested in a trembling voice, as if that might bring Clara to her senses.

"Yes, light! . . . Light . . ." Mr. Dufour echoed.

"No light! No light! I shall smash the lamp to pieces!" Clara shouted, leaping up in anger.

Mr. Dufour rushed out of the room, slamming the door behind him.

"Oh, Clara, Clara!" Adrienne said with a shudder. An abrupt silence fell. They could hear Clara's labored breath. Agitated, she paced back and forth in the cramped salon, collapsed into a chair, and remained there, mute, like a dead woman.

In the silent darkness, in the frightful stuffiness of the little room, they let out deep sighs, which in time dissolved into dull sobbing. All three of them thought of Max and Marie, now perfectly happy, and their strained nerves quivered . . .

II.

TELEGRAMS, picture postcards, and letters arrived from the newlyweds: a telegram from Brussels confirming their safe arrival; a second telegram announcing their departure for Paris; various postcards; and two letters, one for Mr. Dufour and another for all three sisters.

Max and Marie were happy, utterly happy; they had never imagined two people on earth could attain such complete and perfect happiness. "Max is so good, so awfully good and sweet to me," Marie wrote to her sisters-in-law. And Max added underneath, "Who wouldn't be good and sweet to such a darling little angel of a wife!"

"I do hope they haven't forgotten to write to the Aunts," fretted Mr. Dufour.

From Paris came cards and letters with an exhilarated tone. Marie had ordered a new tailor-made dress (as she had planned to do even before her marriage) and it looked splendid, especially since, on the tailor's recommendation, she had selected a hat that matched perfectly. About Paris itself they had no end of stories. Such a magnificent city, a-bustle with activity and joyous life! There you were always in a rush, on your way from one thing to another, your five senses weren't enough to take everything in, and by evening they were sometimes so exhausted that they didn't even go to the theater. Still, they often thought of home and of everyone there. How delighted they had been to read the first letters from papa and the sisters. Papa didn't have to worry; they were in regular correspondence with the Aunts; they had already sent two letters and a number of postcards.

"Don't say too much about all your frivolous doings there in Paris," advised Mr. Dufour.

The sisters received and read those missives with all sorts of emotions and feelings, often contradictory. Sometimes they shared in the newlyweds' joy and exhilaration; at other times, it weighed on them, and the contrast with their own humdrum lives was keen and biting. Then they sometimes had the impression that all of Max and Marie's happiness, all their enjoyment, lent them a quality of eternal youth and living freshness, while they, by comparison, felt older and dingier and more desolate than they really were. A powerless, hopeless mood came over them; they felt worn out despite never having lived; a black horizon closed them in its veil, as it closed the dead earth in its veil of mist and rain in those long, melancholy, downcast December days, so bitterly short and yet so endless.

The spouses traveled on; they had left Paris and were lingering on the Riviera. And the letters they sent from there spoke of wonders, of a Paradise on earth such as no one could imagine who had not truly seen and experienced it. It was a sight to kneel and pray to, possessed of a luxury and wealth far beyond that of Paris, a life of prodigal pleasure as if only millionaires were left in the world. They had also gone to Monte Carlo and played at the Casino, and Max had been lucky, winning three hundred francs.

"The foolishness! The foolishness!" growled Mr. Dufour. "He should never have done it. Shame on him."

"I can certainly see why he did it, and I'd do the same, if I had the opportunity to travel there!" Clara cried out, almost defiantly.

"You would lose your money; all gamblers lose in the end," pessimistically predicted Mr. Dufour.

They went on to Genoa, and to Florence. Picturesque, all most interesting and picturesque, they wrote, but dirty, very dirty. The Italians were dirty people, and untrustworthy at that; you had to watch out when you exchanged money or paid for things. There were often mistakes in the bills, and never in your favor. So they were disappointed in Italy and would not have stayed if it weren't for Rome and the Pope. Rome made little difference to them, to be honest, but the Pope—oh, they had to see him, even if only for a second, and from a distance.

That was their one and only reason for going to Rome. And one day came the letter: a letter of quiet, devout jubilation, for they had seen Him! They had seen him seated on his throne, surrounded by chamberlains and cardinals, dressed all in white, with a white skullcap on his head and a large ring on his finger that shone from a distance like a star. Marie had almost swooned and hardly dared to look up at him, her heart pounding, her eyes misty with tears. But Max had taken a good look and seen that His Holiness was rather short in stature, with thin, sallow features and large, dark eyes. For an moment, His Holiness had looked back, straight at Max. But then, overwhelmed and trembling like a child, Max had lowered his eyes and seen no more. The event had made a lasting impression; tears came to his eyes when he thought of it; he would give his whole trip, with all its pleasures, for that one moment when the Pope had glanced his way. Now they were on their way back. They planned to make another brief stop in Paris, where Marie had a little more shopping to do, and then return home a few weeks later. It was high time, Max wrote. Marie was sometimes very tired, and for the past few days she had not been feeling well. Nothing bad, he reassured them; he would tell them later.

After reading that letter, the sisters were hushed with emotion. The sight of the Pope! It was beyond their power to imagine. It was . . . a reason to rejoice and also to tremble. They listened, as if in a dream, to the words of their father, who was excited to think of the joy that these tidings would bring the Aunts; they endeavored to picture the spectacle as they supposed it must have happened. They saw Marie on her knees in a stately hall, half-swooning, as the Pope rested his dark eyes, for an instant, on their brother. The Pope . . . the Pope . . . they had seen the Pope! They had stood between the same walls; they had breathed the same air. It sanctified them, as it were, in the sisters' eyes; they were now made of more refined stuff; they breathed a higher, cleaner, purer air! And they could hardly imagine— the sisters, that is—how their brother and his wife could bear up under the weight of that distinction, how they could go on with their daily lives like ordinary folk. The reflection of that unparalleled glory dizzied them.

Afternoon came and still they were sitting with the letter in their laps, full of solemn emotion, discussing it ad infinitum, when an old-fashioned carriage rattled up the drive and stopped at the door.

The Aunts! . . . The nieces sprang up in alarm and raced outside. Mr. Dufour was already at the coach door, helping his sisters alight.

"Can it be true?" cried Aunt Clemence, even before she was inside.

"Yes, Aunt, yes, Aunt!" they all echoed.

The Aunts entered; Vreesken, the wizened coachman with his old-fashioned, faded livery hat, drove the old barouche into the carriage house.

"What an honor! What an honor!" Aunt Estelle repeated, with a pious clapping of her hands. Aunt Victoire said nothing, but her pale cheeks rose and fell like a bellows, which in her case was always a sign of the deepest emotion.

They stayed for afternoon coffee with the nieces and spoke of nothing but that weighty, wondrous event.

"Now they must always remember to lead lives of goodness and distinction," Aunt Clemence declared.

"They will, no doubt!" Mr. Dufour assured her.

Aunt Estelle, her hands folded together, nodded in full agreement with her brother's words.

"Only . . . how unfortunate that they traipsed about that shameless city of Paris first!" Aunt Victoire broke in when they least expected it, in a spiteful tone.

They all raised their eyebrows—startled, nearly cringing.

"Pooh-pooh! Pooh-pooh! *Il faut bien que jeunesse se passe*,"[1] Mr. Dufour broke in, trying to smooth things over.

"And that on their way home they plan to stop in Paris again!" Aunt Victoire grumbled on.

A brief silence fell. Something oppressive and suffocating descended on them, as it were. Aunt Victoire huffed, audibly; Aunt Estelle moved her folded hands nervously back and forth, and Aunt Clemence's angular face took on a hard, tight expression.

"Victoire may take it a little too severely," she said, "but I cannot deny that, as she says, it is somewhat inappropriate to enter into the presence of His Holiness between two visits to a place as rotten to the core as Paris."

"Buh . . . buh . . . buh . . ." spluttered Mr. Dufour.

---

1 One must make allowances for youth.

The nieces said nothing more, no longer daring to speak. Aunt Victoire was huffing away. Aunt Estelle looked around with pining, pleading eyes.

"All the same, it's an honor . . . a very great honor all the same," she concluded shyly.

"An honor that will be difficult to live up to," Aunt Clemence proclaimed. "One must hope that Max will now see fit to make certain changes to his life. For instance, his intimate friendship with that Mr. Raymond—a real cad, to put it mildly. We have heard stories . . ."

Adrienne sat bolt upright as if stuck with a pin, batting her eyelids as if staring into unwelcome sunlight. A hot color blazed over her cheeks and soon vanished, leaving her very pale.

"I think we shall soon see the end of that—of their intimacy," replied Mr. Dufour. "At the wedding, Raymond got to know Marie's two West Flemish cousins, the Verstratjes, and now they're practically inseparable."

"That's just it," Aunt Clemence broke in. "Those Verstratjes are a most distasteful pair of drunkards, brawlers, and carousers, and it would be a terrible shame if Max were tangled up with them as well."

Adrienne drew a deep breath. She'd feared she might hear worse. She had seen Raymond strike up that friendship with the Verstratjes; they shared an interest in horses and hunting, and although Adrienne did not care much for the two brothers, she understood the reason for the connection and could find little harm in it. She saw the three of them ride into the village together two or three times a week. The brothers would drop in, as casual as breathing, from their West Flemish village and gallop around with Raymond like a Carnival procession, filling the quiet streets with a tremendous clatter of hooves and bringing the villagers out onto their doorsteps to see. They were not at all agreeable fellows to look at, with their thin, red, sour faces and mean eyes, the type of men who sometimes drank a little too much and got into a scuffle in the pub. There had been a few incidents of that nature, which led to plenty of talk in the village. No doubt that was how the friendship had come to the attention of the Aunts.

This turn of events left Adrienne saddened and disappointed—mostly because of the Aunts' reaction. It left a kind of blot on Marie's side of the family, and therefore on Max too, and his friend Raymond. That alone would give the Aunts more than enough reason to refuse their consent unconditionally if Raymond were ever to set his

sights on her. Those Verstratjes! . . . Adrienne
suffered in silence but could do nothing. What
right would she have? Only once since the wedding had they been to Mr. Dufour's home to pay
their respects. Their manners were rude, and they
seemed uncomfortable in the company of ladies.
Raymond had arrived soon afterwards, and the
three of them had talked at length about horses
while Adrienne looked on, full of hidden emotion and inner trembling. She could hardly keep
her eyes off Raymond and was distressed to realize that the Verstratjes, with their sour eyes, had
noticed that. She breathed a sigh of relief when
they finally left, but in the days that followed she
was hounded and oppressed by the thought that
one of the Verstratjes had discovered her carefully
guarded secret.

The Aunts had risen to go. Martha was sent
scurrying to fetch Vreesken, and not long afterwards he drove up in the old-fashioned carriage,
slumped on his box in his strange livery hat, which
was turning a greenish color.

The Aunts extended limp hands toward their
brother and the nieces, who all accompanied them
to the carriage. Vreesken gave a clumsy salute with
the whip.

The old spinsters groaned with effort as they
climbed in, and the rusty springs contracted with
a screech.

"We hope to receive a visit from Max and his wife soon after they return," Aunt Clemence said in parting.

The nieces nodded, and Mr. Dufour shouted:

"I shall send them to you the moment they are home."

Aunt Victoire pulled the window shut and they rode away in the airless rattletrap, though the day was mild and beautiful, with a glorious sunset in chaotic skies beyond the distant, naked treetops.

III.

JUST before Christmas, one late afternoon close to dusk, Max and Marie returned from their long, delightful honeymoon. They could stay with the Dufours for only a few days; Max was in a hurry to return to his work as a lawyer in the nearby provincial town where he had settled before his marriage.

Mr. Dufour had gone out on urgent business, but the three girls were seated at the window when the carriage, which had gone to pick up the newlyweds from the nearby station, came driving up to the house.

They saw Marie's white-gloved hand wave through the open window, just as they'd seen it last when the couple left on their honeymoon, and the next moment they were all falling into each other's arms, and glad voices of reunion echoed loud in the otherwise dull and silent house.

All three of them fixed their eyes on their sister-in-law and found her much changed. Just what had changed was not so easy to express in words; she had a new aura about her, she looked different, her voice was different, her laugh was different, and her outfit came as a complete surprise: a very fashionable, elegant, brown, tailor-made dress and a small, dark brown hat against which a bright orange ribbon flashed like a spark. It was a charming ensemble, but also quite daring; the sisters would certainly need some time to adjust to it. They thought she seemed thinner, too, and more delicate; they did not think she looked especially well. Max too seemed slightly different; he too seemed thinner, lighter, and more elegant than before, and his face, with its full, dark beard, which had always seemed a little grave and solemn and self-important, now showed distinct marks of self-satisfaction and solemnity; a sense of grave responsibility drew its double groove on his furrowed brow, while his face, which had grown paler, seemed to wear a ceremonious mask. He waited sedately for the first wave of excitement to ebb, and then, the second time Clara mentioned that she did not think Marie looked all that well, he pursed his lips into a cryptic smile and explained, "Perhaps not . . . but it's all part of the . . . circumstances." The sisters turned to him in astonishment. Marie's cheeks turned a fiery red.

"How so . . . what do you mean?" asked Clara, after a pause.

"Well . . . you see . . . it's the sort of thing that happens when one is married," he replied, with a dandyish grin.

The sisters were at a loss for words; they stared intently at Marie, who smiled too, as tender tears welled up in her eyes.

"Maybe . . ." she whispered shyly, lowering her face.

"So soon!" the sisters cried out in surprise, almost distressed.

They could not get over it. They stared at Marie as if at some strange and almost monstrous marvel. Clara's face had tense, hard lines and her cheeks were burning. Adrienne's mouth was half open and her eyes were gleaming. Edmée, who had been feeling poorly again for the past few days, made a pale, sour face and looked away, as if embarrassed.

The door opened and Mr. Dufour came in. He'd rushed back to see them; he hurried over to his son and daughter-in-law and enfolded them in a clumsy embrace. He was very emotional. His hands were shaking, and his watery blue eyes were overflowing with tears, which he kept stubbornly trying to blink away.

"All is well, then? All is well?" he kept repeating, in a trembling voice. Then he noticed the strange looks on everyone's faces and inquired, with a sudden hint of fear:

"No unpleasantness, I trust . . . ?"

They told him the probable news.

He practically reeled with surprise. His eyes widened and his tall form recoiled, as if from some oncoming threat. Then he broke into shrill, nervous laughter that racked his frame.

"Papa, really!" Clara protested, as if his laughter were somehow improper.

He soon pulled himself together, composed his features, and put on a grave, weighty face.

"Don't forget to inform the Aunts as soon as possible," he urged them.

"Of course! Straight away tomorrow," said Max.

They all sat down, and Max started to tell them about the long, wonderful trip. His enthusiasm was irrepressible . . .

IV.

AT the stroke of three, Mr. Dufour's coach-man Floorke drove up in the closed landau. Max helped Marie and his sisters climb in and took a seat on the box, next to the coachman. Mr. Dufour did not join them; there wasn't room in the carriage, and he did not deem his presence absolutely necessary.

They rode out to visit the Aunts . . .

Not one of them was looking forward to it in the least, but they all sensed and understood that the visit could not be put off a day longer—they had no choice.

Marie and the three sisters were all dressed in a plain, subdued style, the sisters in gray and black and Marie in her brown suit and the small, dark brown hat with the bright orange bow. Clara and Edmée had eyed the orange bow with concern. "Wouldn't it be better to take it off?" Clara had suggested.

"Why?" said Marie, anything but pleased with the idea.

"Because the Aunts . . . they're rather particular about that sort of thing."

"It would simply ruin the effect of the hat; that dash of color is what makes the outfit complete."

Adrienne sided with her sister-in-law, but the others disagreed. This exchange of views came close to spoiling the mood, until Max intervened, declaring that the bow would remain. Clara and Edmée both made sour faces and complained that Max was being a bit high-handed, sticking his nose into things he did not understand. But this passing cloud of resentment had soon sailed by, and they rode out in perfect harmony to see the Aunts.

"But how ever shall I tell her? And when?" asked Marie for the hundredth time.

"When the moment is right!" replied Clara, likewise for the hundredth time.

"But suppose it never is?"

Yes . . . she had no answer to that. It was a prickly business. The news had to be told, one way or another. But none of them could predict how the Aunts would take it.

They drove through the subdued winter land-scape of melancholy, leafless trees under a gray sky. The fields lay drab and barren and hordes of cawing black crows flocked over them, sometimes settling on the damp, glistening soil like large, whirling flakes of ash. The scattered farmhouses, pressed into the ground, as it were, by their thatched roofs, were like gloomy, deserted islands in a cheerless sea. How desolate and melancholy it all looked, and how it weighed on the spirits of the two who had just returned from the laughing, sunny lands! Marie breathed a sigh of relief when they finally passed out of those low, muddy fields into drier, brighter country and saw the first pine woods. From there they could make out the large village with stumpy towers where the Aunts lived. Max glanced back from the box and pointed it out to his wife with a smile. She smiled back, but oh, how happy she would be when that visit was over.

They arrived at the village. Instead of driving into it, they turned off to the right, and a few minutes later they were rolling through the open gate of the Aunts' home. Marie caught a glimpse of the two-story house, painted white with pale green shutters, and of the garden in its winter bareness, framed by a wide rectangular moat.

Max hopped off the box and rang the bell. Almost at once, the old kitchen maid Eemlie opened the door.

"Are the Aunts in?" Max asked, for the sake of propriety; he knew they were.

"Ay, Mester Max, come straight on in; welcome ter all of yer!" Eemlie replied with a friendly smile and a humble bow.

The ladies stepped out of the carriage, and Eemlie and Max helped them with their coats. Then Eemlie pushed open a door in the entrance hall, and they proceeded into the parlor.

The Aunts, who had been sitting with their needlework by the wide low window looking out onto the garden, all rose from their seats. Aunt Clemence, being the eldest, took three steps toward the visitors; Aunt Estelle and Aunt Victoire remained for the moment with their hands resting on the backs of their armchairs.

"Welcome, welcome," said Aunt Clemence, and Aunt Estelle and Aunt Victoire echoed, "Welcome, welcome."

They all shook hands and exchanged friendly smiles, but there were no embraces.

"Sit yersen down, sit yersen down," said Eemlie, casual but respectful, pulling up a few extra chairs. They all sat down and started talking.

"The weather's rather fine, isn't it?" Aunt Clemence said.

"Very fine, very fine!" they confirmed in chorus.

"And how was the trip here?"

"Very good, Aunt, very good."

Aunt Clemence's sharp eyes bored into the young couple as she asked the question. Straight away, she noticed the orange ribbon on Marie's hat. Her hand flew up in what looked like surprise, but she made no comment. When she looked again, the other two Aunts followed her gaze. Aunt Estelle gave a sweet smile and unconsciously folded her hands together; Aunt Victoire turned her head away and appeared to huff.

"Oh, very good, Aunt, the weather is lovely today, and charming views," Max repeated. And producing a packet he had carried in under one arm, he said, as his nervous fingers undid the string, "We have brought each of you a little souvenir from Rome."

The Aunts' eyes gleamed with expectation. They were like three children waking up on St. Nicholas's Day. Max carefully unfolded the paper to reveal three large, magnificent rosaries with silver medals and three beautiful portraits of His Holiness the Pope.

"For you, Aunt Clemence; for you, Aunt Estelle; and for you, Aunt Victoire," he said, handing out the presents.

The three spinsters' cheeks burned with emotion, an unexpected, youthful flush that gave their withered features an almost cheerful cast. It was as if Max were handing over three love letters.

"Oh! . . . It's too much, it's too much!" Aunt Clemence sputtered, truly touched. Aunt Estelle could not speak; she had tears in her eyes. Aunt Victoire's face twisted into a hideous grin, like an idiot's.

They held up the rosaries, marveling at the little beads and the little medals, their eyes moist with emotion, and gazing at the beautiful photographs in long, still contemplation, their lips trembling.

"The rosaries were blessed by the Holy Father," Max declared in a low, solemn voice.

"Oh . . . oh . . . oh . . ." The Aunts let out muffled gasps.

Then Aunt Victoire gave Max a piercing look.

"Only . . . how unfortunate that you have no present for Eemlie," she said.

"Oh, I'll show you what I've brought her, Aunt," Max crowed. With an elated look, he rummaged through his pocket and pulled out another rosary, much smaller and less impressive than the ones for the Aunts, but still quite pretty, with little copper medals instead of silver ones.

"And this one was blessed by the Holy Father too?" Aunt Estelle asked, in a transport of emotion.

"Of course, Aunt! Why, of course!" Max gravely replied.

"Eemlie . . . Eemlie . . . get yerself in 'ere!" Aunt Clemence shouted, pushing the door half open.

✳

The old kitchen maid came in, startled by the cries of excitement, and stared about her with a quizzical look.

"Eemlie, 'ere's summat I've brought from Rome for ye," Max said with a smile. "Look! The paternoster—blessed afore my eyes by His Holiness the Pope!"

The elderly maid's coarse hands, which she had been wiping off distractedly on her apron, began to shake violently. Her eyes and mouth went round, and she let out a gasp that seemed to well from the depths of her being. The next moment, her face turned white, and she began to wail and moan:

"Blessed by 'is 'Oliness the Pope . . . but Mester Max . . . I dunna dare ter touch it . . . I have no right ter touch it . . . don' make a mock o' me, Mester Max . . ." And she fell into a fit of sobbing.

"Tut, tut, Eemlie, o' course ye can touch it," Aunt Clemence insisted. Yet she too was so overcome with emotion that she could no longer contain herself and burst into her own wild tears.

Then a madness seemed to descend on the spinsters' house. Aunt Clemence set off Aunt Estelle; Aunt Estelle, Aunt Victoire; and soon it spread to the nieces and Marie and even Max, as hard as he tried to maintain his composure. All the women were gasping and wailing hysterically, as if struck by some unprecedented disaster; and as if each of them were really crying over some secret, private suffering that could not find expression any other way.

Aunt Clemence calmed down first. She confessed that it was absurd to wail when there was every reason to be happy; with an effort of will, she wiped away her tears; and she told Eemlie to hurry and set the table for coffee. This very welcome distraction brought the smiles back to their faces, and they picked up the thread of their conversation. Only Edmée, with her poor health, went on crying in silence for some time afterwards.

Eemlie made haste, and soon they were all seated at the round table by the broad, low windows with a view of the garden. While Eemlie poured the coffee, the Aunts brought around the trays laden with appetizing currant buns and savory pies.

"And now," said Aunt Clemence, pinning Max and Marie with her gaze, "your vacation is over and you will return to your serious lives, won't you?"

"Of course, Aunt. Three or four days from now I'll be knee-deep in work again," Max replied.

"You will have to show some serious application now," Aunt Clemence said. "You're not a bachelor anymore; you will have a family of your own to provide for."

Marie shot Max a questioning look. It was now or never: this was the moment to tell the Aunts the happy news that she was expecting. Her trembling lips were poised to tell all, but she preferred for Max to say it. He squirmed in his chair and lowered his eyes gravely. But instead of the words that Marie expected, he merely responded in a toneless voice, "That's for certain, Aunt Clemence. Of course . . . of course."

Marie, and with her the sisters, let out an involuntary sigh of deep disappointment. Beneath his condescending, self-confident exterior, how frightened Max was of the Aunts!

"For example," Aunt Clemence continued mercilessly, "those shooting parties and that horseback riding with that Mr. Raymond. I'm sure it won't be easy to find time for all that anymore, now will it?"

"Ha! . . . I fear you are right, Aunt. I may no longer have much opportunity for those sorts of things."

There was a brief silence. An oppressive mood weighed vaguely on the group. The unexpected mention of Raymond's name had made Adrienne's cheeks blaze with color, which soon receded, leaving her pale. No one had noticed, but her heart was still beating like a clock.

"*Du reste,*" Aunt Clemence continued in French, because Eemlie had just come in with a fresh pot of coffee, "*il a trouvé de nouveaux compagnons, ces cousins à vous, Marie, qui sont venus à votre diner de noce et qu'on voit maintenant régulièrement avec lui dans le village.*"[1]

"*Oui, je sais, ma tante,*" Marie replied in embarrassment, feeling as if she were expected to apologize for her cousins.

"By all accounts, they are not especially admirable young fellows," Aunt Clemence continued as soon as the maid had left. "In your place, Marie, I would not seek out their company."

"No, Aunt, I wasn't planning to, but it would have been hard not to invite them to the wedding," Marie replied meekly.

---

1 "Besides, he has found new companions, those cousins of yours, Marie, who were at your wedding dinner and are seen regularly with him in the village." Marie replies, "Yes, I know, Aunt."

The sisters sat in oppressive silence, like statues, and Max tugged nervously at his beard. The moment to reveal their great secret seemed to have passed, never to return—yet it had to be done. The Aunts would never forgive them if they heard it from anyone else, at second hand. If only it could wait until another day! But when? They might not see the Aunts again for months.

Max gathered all his courage, coughed, and said, with a slight tremor in his voice:

"In any case, it appears we shan't receive many guests for the next few months, because . . . Marie . . . it seems there's something on the way . . . if you take my meaning . . . that is . . . things could always change, of course . . . but I do believe . . . you see . . ."

He was tangled up in his sentences; he turned red and then pale; his smile was foolish and tormented, overcome as he was by the six wide eyes with which the three dumbfounded Aunts transfixed him.

"You mean to say that . . . that . . . that there is already a child on the way?!" Aunt Clemence finally stuttered, in a dazed voice.

"Well, it would seem so, Aunt."

The six eyes turned from Max to transfix Marie, who bowed her head with burning cheeks.

"I . . . I do believe so too," she stammered.

There followed a long interlude of utter silence. It was as if a gigantic stone had been hurled into still water with a splash and was now on its slow descent into the depths. Aunt Clemence looked from one to the other with sharp, staring eyes that seemed to hold the reflections of mysterious thoughts and feelings. A very light red tinged her normally dull cheeks. Aunt Estelle's head was tipped to the left and she wore a strange expression, as if she'd received some news she would rather not have heard. And Aunt Victoire, who had made a motion as if to rise from her chair, had turned almost frightfully pale, with deeper wrinkles and grooves in her shriveled face and nervous twitches of her mouth, which seemed to want to huff and could not huff. The nieces sat as straight and motionless as statues; one might well have thought they were no longer alive.

"It is your decision . . . entirely your decision . . . but so soon . . . so soon . . ." were the words Aunt Clemence expelled through her thin lips at last, with a disapproving shake of the head.

"Yes . . . yes . . . what can you do . . . so it goes . . ." Max prattled.

Aunt Estelle nodded gently and repeatedly. She seemed to have recovered a bit from her initial shock; she seemed to understand, to excuse, to forgive. She cast a worried look at Aunt Victoire, seated next to her, who was still making fruitless attempts to huff or vocalize.

Aunt Clemence had collected herself. A harsh fold formed around her thin lips; her eyes were screwed tight; and her stern face had regained its habitual tension.

"Above all . . . Above all . . ." she whispered in a tone between warning and reprimand, as if the subject were not quite fit for polite society, "not a word of this to the maid. She has such a loose tongue, and there's really no need for her to go spreading that sort of news all over the village. Shall we go for a stroll in the garden?"

They rose from the table, and it came as a great relief to them all. Wide-brimmed hats were placed on heads, cloaks draped over shoulders; they went outside through the glass door and ambled along the gravel paths.

Max took the lead, with Marie, who was crying. "It's as if we'd committed a crime," she moaned. He took her hand and gave a gentle squeeze, and did his best to console her.

"Oh, what do you expect? Old maiden aunts like them—they can't imagine it," he reassured her.

"They act so devout—and they are," Marie went on. "But how can they reconcile their sheer pigheadedness in this case with the words of the Lord, 'Be fruitful and multiply'?"

"Ah, well, this too shall pass," Max said soothingly. "Think of it: three old, dried-up sisters, never, but never, touched or caressed by a man! Come, kiss me quick!"

He pulled her behind a bank of rhododendrons and took her passionately in his arms.

"Watch out, they'd be furious if they knew!" she whispered in fright, pushing him away.

The Aunts and the nieces followed, six dark silhouettes on the light gravel path that was lined with conical growths. The garden's many varieties of spruce trees created a churchyard atmosphere, and the six severe maidens strolling through it were like six widows grieving for some irretrievable happiness. On the bare limb of a leafless beech tree sat a starling, singing its brief song, half-complaint and half-mockery, and at the feet of the sisters and Aunts, a sociable robin hopped along with them, its feet as fine and straight as rods of glass, its eyes glinting around like beads, its breast stained with its bib, as red as passion and death. A hazy sun set; a gray winter mist came creeping in.

"It must be about time for us to return home," Clara said. And she called out to Max, at the back of the garden, "Max, it's time. It's getting dark."

Floorke, who'd had coffee in the kitchen with Eemlie, was waiting in front of the house with the carriage. The nieces and Marie said farewell to the Aunts and stepped in. Max clambered up beside Floorke on the box, as he had on the way there.

The three Aunts stood and watched them go. Aunt Clemence was smiling with an air of reserved self-satisfaction, Aunt Estelle wore a very friendly smile, and Aunt Victoire had finally recovered the ability to huff, and was unmistakably huffing as she stared at them with her sour, peevish face and muttered something between half-closed lips about driving carefully in the dark. Eemlie stood behind her and, from a distance, thanked the visitors again for the beautiful gift; her eyes were moist.

Max had lit a cigar and was puffing away in the cool evening air. His nerves were still agitated; he could not sit still and kept turning to Marie and his sisters in the carriage to say things they could hardly make out.

"What on earth does he want? We can't hear a thing!" they said, laughing. They were gradually cheering up again, now that they could shrug off the weight of the dreaded visit. It was a true relief. Though not at all exuberant by nature, they now felt the need to celebrate their recovered freedom, and they talked and laughed together and screeched with delight at Max on the box, who was striking funny poses, his arms stretched wide as if just released from a straitjacket. Then all at once, he leaned far forward, peering out into the twilight. With an almost immediate whoop of delight, he made Floorke stop the carriage.

"What's going on?" Marie and the girls shouted in surprise. They could see the answer for themselves soon enough, when three men on horseback emerged from the half-darkness and stopped on the narrower bridle path beside the landau.

"Oh, God!" Adrienne cried aloud, in spite of herself.

It was Raymond with Marie's two cousins, the Verstratjes!

Max had jumped off the box and was giving his friend a hearty handshake. "Where are you headed at this hour?" the ladies heard him ask.

"Just seeing off Edmond and Evarist," Raymond replied with a smile.

Clara opened one of the carriage windows and stuck out her head.

"Mademoiselle," Raymond said, with a polite bow. Noticing the vague shapes of the other women, he greeted them too, doffing his hat. The Verstratjes, behind him, followed his example in their clumsy, boorish way. Marie drew back into the depths of the carriage so that she wouldn't have to speak to her cousins.

"How was your trip?" Raymond asked.

"Oh, fine," said Max. "I'll tell you all about it later. But, I say, is that a new horse you have there?"

"Yes, and a remarkable one!" Raymond said, beaming. "You simply can't imagine, old bean! Will you have a go?"

"Ha! You can be sure of it, but not now, don't you know!" Max replied with a grin. "Tell you what, I'll pay you a visit soon."

"Yes, you must, you must!"

The Verstratjes were looking a little impatient. Their horses stamped and were eager to go home. It was getting late, and dark.

"Right," Raymond said to the Verstratjes, "you chaps know the way from here, don't you? You go on home, and I'll stay with the carriage for a bit."

Adrienne, who was seated opposite Clara with burning cheeks, now in turn stuck her head through the window. She saw Raymond on his gray, and her admiring gaze seemed to thank him for his words. She felt just as if he'd abandoned his friends for her and her alone, so that the two of them could ride back together. It did not for a moment occur to her that Raymond, with a horse lover's vanity, might simply have wanted to show off his fine new steed to Max. She gazed at him with a warm smile, until she noticed with a jolt that one of the Verstratjes—the same one who, earlier, had half-discovered her secret—was looking on from his saddle in the dusk with a leer and a chuckle. She withdrew as fast as she could into the shadowy interior of the landau, as Raymond swiftly turned his horse around and said goodbye to the Verstratjes. The two brothers lifted their riding crops in an awkward farewell to the ladies, spurred their horses on, and vanished into the darkness.

The landau rolled on down the cobbled road with a muffled rattle, and Raymond rode beside it along the bridle path, like a guard of honor. Even in the gathering dusk, Adrienne could see him clearly, and she never took her eyes off him. The way he rode, so manly and so at ease in the saddle! It was as if he were seated in an armchair. He was so completely at one with his fine horse. She saw the faint gleam of the gray's smooth back, and its lovely long silvery tail swept back and forth, slow and graceful, as the horse kept up its regular trot. She could tell what a pleasure it must be to ride that way. The sight was somehow noble, full of quiet strength and beauty, and made a potent impression on her. She could not take her fascinated eyes off it, and after a while what she saw seemed almost miraculous: something out of a dream or a fairy tale, a magic spell in which he moved, like an almost unreal apparition. What was it? What was happening to him and his horse? She saw the pale glow of the gray's back, which seemed to have turned to matte bronze, and the glints of brass in the silvery tail, while the silhouette of the rider himself was edged on the right with a delicate, wavering line of copper. When she happened to glance over her shoulder, through the rear window of the carriage, she saw the miracle: it was the full moon, glowing dull orange as it rose low in the East and cast its slanted light on the horse and rider. Oh, look how beautiful . . . how beautiful! Adrienne could not suppress her jubilation and scarcely knew herself what she most admired: the storybook knight or the enchantment of the rising moon. It melted into one perfect harmony of beauty, bringing tears to her eyes.

Max, on the box, felt his own sort of admiration for the horse and its rider; he and Raymond discussed their impressions as they traveled on. As the moon rose higher, its light turning whiter, the contours of the horse and rider grew clearer. A very light veil of mist came creeping up out of the ground, making him look as if he were riding through a dreamy lake; the cadence of the hooves was vaguely like the sound of oars. How beautiful and poetic all this was, how moving! Adrienne's soul rejoiced and trembled. How different the life in one person from the life in another! That dull, oppressive feeling back there, at the Aunts' house, and here, that freshness, that freedom, that hearty strength! Swayed by these musings, she felt she was riding with that handsome horseman. She closed her eyes and felt herself rise and fall in a rhythm of heavenly bliss.

When she opened her eyes again, the carriage had stopped in front of Mr. Dufour's house, and she heard Raymond's voice bid Max a cheerful goodbye. They exchanged a few more words, and then he came to the window and bid farewell to the ladies, the leather of his saddle creaking as he bent toward them. He politely turned down the invitation to come inside for a short visit, saying the hour was too late for him. With a dashing wave of the arm, he straightened up again in his stirrups and, tipping his hat one last time, vanished into the night.

To Adrienne, it seemed he had taken her life with him.

V.

AT seven in the morning, his usual hour, Raymond rose from his bed. After shaving and washing, he pulled on his pants and his large leather boots, as he did each morning. It wasn't as if each morning he went out riding, but each morning he was prepared for the possibility. What is more, he remained in that outfit all day. He was like a soldier putting on his uniform, without a second thought. It was unthinkable for him to dress any other way.

He opened the shutters along two walls of his room, and through the four windows, the mild gray light of the winter morning poured in. On both sides of the room, he glanced outdoors. It was a fresh, bracing morning, with silvery frost on the grass and trees. The temperature had dipped just below freezing; on the water of the wide moat around the house lay a very thin crust of ice, cracking open in places under the thrash and waggle of the ducklings. The large orchard seemed laden with bouquets of strange, white blossoms, and the long stalls, stables, and barns were dreaming away beneath a bluish sky, which drew the warmth of the animals out and up.

Raymond whistled a tune and hummed a song. He put on his sport coat, ran his fingers over his moustache, and scrutinized himself in the mirror. He was pleased with what he saw there. He had slept soundly and looked robust and full of life. He felt that he wore his thirty-seven years very well, with little or no wear and tear. That was thanks to sports and the healthy country life. Sports, he thought . . . and staying unmarried! He smiled. Why would he want to marry, anyway? Later, maybe. For now, his young, single life was still far too lusty and full of pleasures.

He bounded downstairs to his dining room, where the table was set for breakfast. The dogs were waiting for him, as usual, and came to greet him. Ooh-ooh, the large St. Bernard, wagged his tail sedately and laid his heavy head with blood-shot eyes on Raymond's arm. But Impikoko, the Irish terrier, was much more demonstrative in his affections; he jumped almost as high as his master's face and laughed with delight, like a human, baring all his fine strong white teeth. Raymond petted them, dividing his attention between the two; but Impikoko was jealous of Ooh-ooh. Wanting all the love to himself, the little dog bit the good-natured hulk in his thick, strong tail, as if to drag him off his master. Then the big dog growled at the little one, which leapt to safety, and soon they were all rolling around the floor together, until Manse, the kitchen maid, came in with breakfast and asserted her unchallenged authority.

"Are ye mankin' abaht with those flamin' dogs again?" was her usual morning salutation. Then she turned on the dogs: "Goo on, ye gret good-for-nowt, sluther off! And ye little thing, if ye put yer clarty paws on my tablecloth once more . . . !"

"But Manse, there's nowt amiss with sayin' good mornin', is there?" Raymond said with a smile.

"Gerraway wi' ye an' all yer mischief!" Manse grumbled. "Enough rammel, sit ye down an' eat yer breakfast."

Manse was fifty-five years old and had grown up in that house and served Raymond's parents. She had seen Raymond born and seen his parents die. To her, Raymond was still the little boy she had played with when he was in his cradle. She showed not a shred of deference toward him, but was on the most familiar of terms with him, doling out advice and scolding him as if he were her own son. On top of all that, she was as fond of him as his dogs were and defended his interests as if they were her own. He was free to go out riding and hunting as often as he pleased; she ran the farm like a man, overseeing and managing everything. She had a round face—with extraordinarily bright eyes, a wondrous shade of light brown, nearly yellow, which seemed to shine a light on a person's secrets—and a slight limp, which made her movements no less quick.

"Nar then, hurry up, eat an' drink while it's still warm!" she ordered him as if he were a boy.

Raymond sat down and smiled. This brusque familiarity didn't bother him in the least. He was used to it from Manse, and it amused him. For his part, he always enjoyed teasing her.

"Manse," he said in a cheeky tone, as he started to eat, "ah dreamt abaht marryin' agin last night."

"Oh, ye mucky scamp!" she growled.

That was one thing she couldn't abide. She knew he was only teasing, but even so, she couldn't stand it.

"What would ye go marryin' for? Are ye already weary of yer fine young life?" she grumbled, fixing him with a fierce glare. And as she limped back toward the kitchen, she gave him an impertinent poke with her elbow in passing.

"Well, what's th'story? Are ye sure those two youths are stoppin' for dinner again?" she asked.

"An' a drop ter drink," he said.

"Ay, those lads can drink! Ohhh . . . the faces on 'em, red an' blue!" Manse cried, throwing her arms up into the air with a cackle. "Ay, an' ah should know, by all th'saints! Ah mun send Tieldeken ter the butcher afore they come."

"They're on their way, Manse. Ah'll go aht yonder to meet them, see?"

Manse turned around and shouted in the direction of the open door, "Tielde!"

A swift rustle of skirts, and a young girl appeared in the doorway.

"Mornin', Mester Raymond," she said, politely and a little shyly.

"Mornin', Tieldeken," he replied, with a friendly glance over his shoulder.

"Tieldeken, ye mun go ter the butchery," Manse said. "What shall we ax for? Three nice tender steaks?" she went on, turning to her master.

"*Bon*. Very good," he replied.

Manse felt she owed him a few more words of explanation.

"Ah could make a nice bowl o' soup, a thick steak for each o' 'em, then hare pâté, and a little summat sweet for after . . . they'll 'ave nowt ter chunter abaht."

"Nay, nowt, Manse," he acknowledged with a grin.

76

"Ay, but . . . ye're only mankin' abaht again. That willna put yer dinner on th'table!" the maid grumbled. "Well, are ye content?"

"Ah canna imagine owt better, Manse."

Tieldeken, waiting in the doorway, also had a quiet smile on her face. She was a pretty young girl around seventeen years old, one of Manse's nieces; her aunt had taken her on to help out. She had dark hair, red cheeks, and lively brown eyes and was tall and robust for her age.

"Well, y'eard what I said, didna? Utch up, and dunna stay away too long!" Manse said to her niece.

The girl rushed off, and Raymond, done with his breakfast, rose from his chair. He lit a pipe and went outside, accompanied by the dogs, while Manse whisked the dishes off the table.

"Which wine glasses shall ye have?" the maid called after him.

Raymond mulled it over before replying:

"Claret an' burgundy!"

"Yo lads will drink yersen inter th'grave!" the maid screeched.

Raymond laughed and walked on.

He took a deep breath of the sharp winter morning air. The sunlight was already starting to beckon and play through the thin mists; it would be a glorious day, a perfect, bracing day to ride a horse. He went straight to the outbuildings, as he did each morning, for a quick inspection. There was nothing new or troubling to be discovered; the whole life of the farm was as calm and pleasant as ever. He made these rounds merely out of habit, except in the stables, where he spent more time. The cart-horses were already on their way to the fields, but his two fine mounts, the sorrel and the gray, were in their stalls, being carefully combed, brushed, and cared for by Jan, the stable boy.

"All's well, Jan?" he asked out of habit.

"Ye can see for yersen, sir!" Jan answered with a kind of pride.

Jan felt true affection for all his fine animals, no less than his master did. He looked up at their gleaming coats with satisfaction, and when he patted their thighs it was like a caress. As soon as the horses heard Raymond's voice, they turned their heads, whinnied, and gazed at him, their big, beautiful eyes filled with longing.

"Are ye fellas waitin' for yer sugar, then?" Raymond said with an indulgent smile.

They replied in an almost human manner, and he gave it to them, softly stroking their manes. He wrapped his arms around their necks and pressed his cheek to their heads.

"Fox this day, sir, isna 'er?" Jan asked.

"Ay, Jan."

"When's that, then, sir?"

"Ten o'clock. I'm ridin' out yonder ter meet them. Yer stable is ready?"

"As it should be, sir."

Raymond went outside again. He passed through the rolling orchard to the stream. Impikoko followed him, sniffing right and left. Ooh-ooh, who felt he had walked far enough, stood motionless by the stalls, following them with his eyes.

Raymond went only as far as the little bridge. Beyond that, there was nothing more for him to inspect. There the countryside stretched out on either side of the road, like a big, beautiful, wide-open book. That was all in quiet hibernation now, until the day it reawakened and burst into flower and birdsong. He looked at the water. There, too, a thin crust of ice had formed in some places, so soft and fragile that it rocked and rippled with the water below when Impikoko dipped his paws by the damp bank. Raymond checked his watch and headed for home.

The sun broke through the clouds and shone gently on Carvin's light-yellow limewashed walls and gray shutters. It was a strange, hybrid building, broad and strong at its foundations, narrow and tall on the upper floor. It had vaulted cellars like casemates, but at the top was a lantern with views on all sides.

A stone bridge with a kind of steeply arched ornamental gate gave access to the farm proper, which was surrounded by a wide moat like a fortress. It had looked much the same in earlier centuries, when it was a *Tempelhof* whose fearsome occupants could shut themselves inside and stand a siege if they had to. From one wing rose a square tower with a pointed lead roof, which served no real purpose but heightened the overall effect.

He smiled and thought back to how he had teased the old kitchen maid. Marry! . . . would he really ever marry? Forfeit his treasured freedom? Share his authority? The idea did not tempt him in the least. He still felt so free and easy, like a bird in the sky. Living alone, you could do as you pleased, without anyone to disapprove or even notice. You got up when you liked, went around in your country clothes, ate and drank what you wished, and smoked in every room of the house—even in bed if you felt like it. Once you took a wife, it was goodbye to all that. Yes, you had a woman whenever you liked, you didn't have to walk into town and share her with other blokes; you had a woman of your own, and that was no small advantage, but think of the price!

And yet . . . most fellows ended up marrying, and maybe he would too. Max had done it and appeared to have no regrets. On the other hand, the Verstratjes hadn't married and seemed intent on never taking the plunge. One simply couldn't say what was best. Growing old on your own must be a nasty business. But for him, that was still a very distant prospect; he was in no hurry; he could wait for now and enjoy life.

He went into the house and down to his wine cellar, brought up the bottles he needed, and handed them over to Manse, who would make sure they were at the right temperature. Manse launched into a complicated story about preserving vegetables for the winter; having little interest in listening or responding, he hurried off, telling her it was high time he rode out to meet his friends.

"Take care ye dunna fall with all yer riding!" Manse shouted after him.

The fine sorrel was already saddled, and Jan led him outside. The dogs made excited circles around the horse. Ooh-Ooh was much too slow to follow, and he knew it, but he wanted to see the departure anyway and growled in aggravation, harassed by the little dog's wild leaps and bounds.

Impikoko had not yet been informed whether he would be joining his master, and by the mad, overwrought way he kept pestering Ooh-Ooh, you might have thought it was the bigger dog's decision.

Raymond looked at the two of them and smiled.

"No walkie-walkie," he said, very, very softly.

That alone was enough. The big dog looked at him as if to say, "Are ye havin' us on?" and the little dog flattened his ears tight to his neck, with an expression of sorrow and disappointment on his sweet features as if all possible disasters had come tumbling down upon him. In the depths of his dejection, he seemed almost earless. They were folded against his neck, one over the other, like the little ribbons in back of the coifs of Breton maidens.

"*Yes* walkie-walkie!" Raymond said with a smile, and Impikoko was overjoyed, leaping as high as the horse's mouth, as if to kiss it. In one buoyant motion, Raymond sprang into the saddle and rode away majestically, with Impikoko hopping along ahead of him. Ooh-ooh stood motionless, keeping his eyes on his master as long as he could, and then followed Jan into the stables.

Shortly before one o'clock, Raymond returned to Carvin with his guests. They'd been riding hard and could not have been more ready to do justice to Manse's dinner. The weather had turned misty and chilly again; the thought of the well-spread table by the warm stove was cozy and welcoming.

"Aright, then, co' up and sit yer down by th'stove!" Manse shouted. She was on the same familiar terms with the Verstratjes as with her own master.

"We need summat ter fill th'hole up, Manse. Have ye no smite of bread or potato for us?" the elder brother teased.

"Ay, ay . . . yo' are just the youths to dine on dry bread an' potatoes!" Manse screeched, her eyes flickering with mischief. "Yo know what yo'll 'ave?" she whispered, elbowing her way between the two brothers. "A gret, juicy steak for each o' yo, with hare pâté afterwards. Yo'll love it, lads!" she cried in her shrill voice.

"No soup, Manse? D'ye have no soup for us?" they replied in the same tone, pretending severe disappointment.

"Course there's soup, a belter o' a soup, ye gomerel!" Manse grumbled.

They sat by the fire for a while with outstretched legs, and Tieldeken, in a neat cap and a white apron, brought out glasses of port. It was excellent. The Verstratjes had soon recovered their fiery red hue, which the fresh air had somewhat dispersed, and they took deep drafts from the stubs of their cigars, which they'd come into the house smoking.

They had unusual features, those Verstratjes. At first, you could hardly tell them apart; both were thin and fiery red, with small, bristly mustaches and a spiteful look in their watery blue eyes. They were reminiscent of boiled lobsters. Only after spending some time with them did you detect the outward difference. Edmond, the elder brother, was a little larger and heavier than Evarist, the younger, and the color of his face, seemingly a uniform red, in fact concealed a light purple un-dertone, almost mauve, while the red of his nose had a greenish cast, as if sprayed with some kind of pistachio pollen. Evarist, in contrast, had a black-ish sprinkling in his lobster red. His face gave the impression of having been grated open, salted and peppered, and bandaged up again. Both had bad, smoke-blackened teeth, which accentuated their habitual grins.

Raymond refilled the glasses, and the Verstratjes did not object. For himself, he poured only a small sip. He was a very moderate eater and drinker but enjoyed serving his guests a copious meal.

Manse poked her round face with fierce eyes through the half-open door:

"Well, can ah send the gel in wi' the soup?"

"Ay, Manse, we're ready."

They went to the table and unfolded the napkins. Tieldeken ladled out three formidable portions of soup.

"Ah'm fairly clammed," Edmond declared.

"Ay, so am ah," echoed Evarist.

Their hands were trembling a little, and they slurped slightly. That was what happened to your hands after hours of holding the reins, but it passed once you'd taken a little food and a few glasses of claret. The strangest thing was the Verstratjes' color. By the time the tureen had been emptied, they were both a dark and uniform shade of red. Both the mauve undertone and the pistachio green of Edmond's nose had vanished completely, and the peppering of black on Evarist's cheeks was no longer detectable.

Those more subtle shades returned slowly at first as they went on eating and talking and drinking. The two brothers had something of the chameleon about them.

They talked of horses, and again of horses, and still more of horses. And if you took a good look at them while they talked, you could see their own resemblance to horses: a sort of stiffness around the mouth and lower jaw reminiscent of those animals. Raymond broke in a couple of times with hunting stories, but his friends' attention soon flagged and wandered, until they returned to their inexhaustible equestrian theme. The one brief change of topic was brought on by the arrival of the burgundy and the hare pâté. Ha, ha! That good old Clos de Vougeot, with its clear ruby color and unparalleled "bouquet." The Verstratjes closed their eyes and nibbled as they tasted it. It was better not to speak when one drank such things. By this time they had both reverted to a uniform dark red, and it took quite a while before the return of the mauve, pistachio, and black pepper on grated cheeks. It was as if that magnificent ruby color had seeped into their skin. Edmond let out a short, abrupt laugh, and his watery blue eyes filled with tenderness as he gazed at his half-full glass.

Manse stuck her beaming face through the doorway, uninvited and without knocking, and asked:

"Everythin' ter yer likin', me ducks?"

"Aye, 'tis, Manse!" came the happy shout from all three.

"'Eavens above, yo' lads look red! Yo'll eat an' drink yersen inter a fit!" she hooted, clapping her hands together. And laughing, she limped away again. Tieldeken was laughing too, but modestly and quietly, as she watched from the corner.

"Would ye have yer coffee?" Manse asked, peeping through the door again.

"Ay ay, co' up!"

Raymond rose and fetched the cigars and liqueurs from a cabinet. Each of them took a fat Havana.

Edmond was smiling to himself, his eyes on his glass. He seemed to be having an entertaining thought that he chose not to express in words.

"You're enjoying yourself, I believe," Raymond said, noticing his quiet amusement.

"Oh, a bit . . ." the elder Verstratje said with a snigger. "Just thinking of Max, who's married now."

"And well married, too," Raymond replied earnestly. The Verstratjes grinned.

"Of course," the elder continued, "well married, but married all the same. What's his fine young life worth to him now? He's too busy these days for riding. For all we know the little missus may not allow it; we can't even be certain we'll see him at the next shooting party. He's in her clutches now, but good."

A brief silence fell. Tieldeken went to and fro, serving them. Raymond waited until she had left and said, "Still, I do believe he's happy."

Edmond leered at him. "Maybe one day you will be so happy," he scoffed.

"How so?" Raymond asked.

"I've got eyes in my head. I happened to notice . . . something," Edmond answered, smirking.

"Something about me?" Raymond cried.

"Not *about* you, but *for* you . . . !"

"Now your meaning escapes me entirely," Raymond said.

"Well, nothing escapes me!" the drunkard replied, and his smirk turned sinister. He leaned in, with a glance at the kitchen door, and whispered to Raymond:

"Adrienne Dufour . . . I've seen how she gawks at you, first at the wedding, and later, when we came upon her in the carriage. The look in her eyes tells me enough. Watch out, old bean!"

Raymond looked back and forth from one to the other, his eyes round with stupefaction. It came out of nowhere; he thought they were pulling his leg. But the younger Verstratje was laughing as hard as the elder and confessed that he had seen it too. Yes, yes, it was true, she was in love with him, she was his if he wanted her.

"You're round the bend, both of you!" Raymond said heatedly, shrugging his shoulders. "Come on, drink up, and we'll talk about something else."

"You see, it's true! He's scared to hear it!" the Verstratjes jeered.

"I say, would you lower your voices, please," Raymond said, pointing meaningfully at the kitchen door.

His warning came just in time. The door opened, and Manse's full, round face called out to them:

"Enough hot coffee, me ducks?"

"Aye, aye, more than enough!" Raymond said, dismissing her with a mechanical wave of his hand.

Evening was slowly descending, bathing the old-fashioned dining room in soft shades of gray. A gloom fell over the furniture; a large set of trophy antlers on an antique cupboard cast its twisted silhouette, dark and almost tragic, against the light wall. The visages of the Verstratjes, who were seated with their backs to the windows, were black with dark redness. No expression could be seen any longer on their features, and the red tips of their cigars were like the outward glow of the fire that burned within them. The elder brother looked up to where gentle swipes of gray and red mingled in the western sky, and said, half serious, half joking:

"Anyway, I expect we may hear more about that later, but now we must be on our way. Will you see us off, Raymond?"

"I'll ride out with you . . . a little way. Manse . . . Manse . . . !"

"Ridin' out? Prepare th'orses?" asked the maid, who had made a quick entrance.

89

"Aye, an' tell Jan ah'll take th'dapple gray.

Manse went off at a fast limp, and the Verstratjes consented to one last glass. Then they all stood up and went to the stable.

Impikoko was invited along for a "walkie-walkie." Ooh-Ooh stood motionless and watched them go. The Verstratjes, with fresh cigars in their mouths, looked like rockets. Raymond was graver than usual and looked almost pale beside them, on his pale, handsome gray . . .

He did not ride quite as far as he normally did. Less than half an hour later, he had said farewell to his friends and was returning quietly, at a slow walk, in the twilight.

Well, well . . . Adrienne Dufour! . . . . Whatever had given the Verstratjes that idea? . . . How had they noticed a thing like that, or thought they'd noticed it, when he himself had not suspected in the least? . . . Was it really true, as they had said, or just a tall tale? . . . No, Raymond felt instinctively that they really had noticed something . . . that there truly was something going on.

It gave him a strange, unfamiliar feeling. It brought a sense of well-being and, at the same time, rattled his nerves. It puffed him up like a sweet compliment, but he instantly had the impression that some of the wide, fine freedom of his life was already slipping away. He was flattered, and he was furious. And now that he thought about it more deeply, memories came to mind of details he hadn't noticed at first, which now took on a sudden and deep significance to him. Yes, that afternoon, when she'd sat across from him at the wedding dinner, how she had stared at him the whole time, taking an interest in everything he said and did! And that evening, too, more recently, when he and the Verstratjes had run into Max and his sisters going home in the carriage from their visit to the Aunts, yes, she had looked at him in the same strange way then, so strange—as he thought about it, he could feel it still. It had been an evening like this one, with a full, dull orange moon rising low in the East, and in his mind's eye he once again saw the color shoot to her pale cheeks and that curious, striking look come into her eyes . . . How strange it all was, how unexpected, and how absurd!

Adrienne Dufour! . . . In his mind she stood before him, rising as it were from the thin, moonlit mist, and her arrival was not unwelcome; he greeted her apparition with a warm, friendly smile. She was far from unattractive, with her slender figure, her flowing waves of blonde hair, and her gentle blue eyes. Adrienne was by far the prettiest of the three sisters, and he suspected she was also the sweetest, the friendliest, and the most adorable. Yes, she was the kind of woman you might fall in love with and be happy with. Had he already fallen in love with her, or could he? . . . Oh, it was all so strange and absurd, so unexpected, so entirely out of the blue! . . . A woman, a woman at Carvin, he couldn't imagine! What would Manse think, and Tieldeken, and even Ooh-Ooh and Impikoko? Would Manse and Tieldeken give notice at once, weeping and wailing as if some unforeseen, unmerited disaster had befallen them? Or would they approve, and be glad, and wish him every happiness, and promise to stay as devoted to him as ever? He couldn't say, he had no idea, his imagination failed him.

That was the mood in which he returned to Carvin. He was in the habit of reading the newspaper in the evening and catching up on correspondence if necessary. But somehow he couldn't; the words he read meant nothing to him, and his pen lay idle on the paper. His thoughts trailed off into daydreams. He sat smoking, his eyes absently following the blue circles as he pondered.

Pushing open the door, Manse broke into his reverie:

"What'll ye sup upon this evenin'?"

He winced. Supper! He had not the least appetite for anything.

"Nowt," he replied.

"'Tha'll niver 'ave nowt!" Manse cried in outrage. "Or are ye feelin' poorly?" she added in a milder voice, somewhat concerned.

"Ah, nay," he said, "but ah—ah've lost my appetite," he said.

"Ye canna lose yer appetite!" she shouted in a tone of command. "Ah'll go an' scramble some heggs for ye this minute. That's fillin', see, and easy on the innards!" And without waiting for his yes or no, she limped back to the kitchen.

"Yer heggs, sir," said Tieldeken, serving the dish with a gentle, encouraging smile.

"Ah suppose ah mun eat 'em, will ah or no," he said with a chuckle, shrugging his shoulders.

"One little bite, sir. T'will do ye good," said the young girl, with friendly insistence. He looked up at her and smiled. How kind of her to care for him as she did. He gave her a friendly nod and picked up his fork.

"He mun eat! He mun eat 'em all up!" came the voice of Manse, who had stealthily opened the door again.

He ate, and when his coffee arrived, he stretched out in his armchair and lit a cigar. He felt a winter loneliness stealing over him. Now he had nothing more to do and no interest in taking up anything. And why should he? Was he to walk to the village again for another round of cards or billiards at the Trading House with Mr. Dufour and the other village worthies? He didn't feel like it. It was always the same; a tedious game and pointless conversation. What, then? Go back to his paper, or read a book! Bah! The paper was stuffed with lies, and a book from his small shelf of light novels, that was the very essence of un-truth; writers twisted everything. He couldn't get involved in that.

He was bored. It was the first time he had ever felt there was something he lacked and that he was bored. How had it happened? Was it all because of what the Verstratjes had told him, so casually, that afternoon? Was that . . . how stupid . . . how silly . . . how childish . . . was it that feeble story about Adrienne Dufour? . . . Adrienne Dufour! . . . Back to Adrienne Dufour again! What was wrong with him? What did he care about her? He couldn't have fallen in love with Adrienne Dufour from one moment to the next, just because of a few stray words from the Verstratjes, when he had never spared a thought for her before! . . . Irritated, he got up, reached for the bell, and rang it. Soon Tieldeken was standing before him with a smile.

"Tieldeken, would ye ax Manse to fix me a rum grog with a slice o' lemon?"

"Ay, sir, very good."

An instant later, Manse herself, followed by Tieldeken, brought him the rum grog.

"Ye mun be made-up wi' a chill!" she cried accusingly. "Serves ye right for gaddin' abaht on 'orses in th'cold."

"Go on an' give it 'ere, Manse. Ah'll soon be right as rain," he said with a smile.

The grog did him good. An invigorating warmth coursed through his body, and his cigar tasted much better. He stretched his feet out toward the hearth, where Impikoko and Ooh-Ooh were already snoring away. What good people he had around him, and how lucky he was compared so many others! Old Manse might be overbearing and impertinent at times, but she took such good care of him and was as loyal as a hound! And Tieldeken, that sweet girl, so isolated there at Carvin, without anyone her own age, without any diversions, year in, year out! She never complained; she was contented and seemed to want for nothing.

He sipped from his glass, shook his head, and was filled with affection. Those good people lived for him and depended on him for their living. He had a kind of moral duty toward them; he had no right to do anything that might disturb their peaceful lives. They were such innocents; they had complete confidence in him, almost like Impikoko and Ooh-Ooh, who could never understand if he changed the rules they lived by, if he had to start ordering them to stop doing what they had always been perfectly free to do before. No, no, there could be no change in his life. Life was good to all of them as it was, and that was how it should stay, for years and years to come.

"Well!" said Manse, pushing open the door. "Are ye feelin' a bit better now?"

"Much better, Manse, it did me a world o' good. Ye mun fix two more glasses o' th'same, for th'two o' you."

"Ah, dunna tease me, duck! We'd be three sheets ter th'wind!" Manse hooted, her eyes sparkling with excitement.

"Come, come, none 'o yer no's, ye mun drink!" he insisted.

"Ye means it, now? Well, if ye're sure . . ." And screeching with laughter, Manse limped back to the kitchen to fix two more glasses.

"Ter yer 'ealth, sir!" Manse and Tieldeken toasted him.

He clinked his glass against theirs and they drank, laughing. Tieldeken soon turned scarlet and was seized by a coughing fit. It had gone down the wrong way.

"Ye munna be so greedy when ye drink," Manse grumbled.

96

But a moment later, Manse herself doubled over with coughing, and the two of them made their way back to the kitchen, bent over and convulsing, holding their glasses stiffly out in front of them, laughing and coughing all at once, a little embarrassed about making such a scene in the presence of their master.

It had woken the dogs, who came to rub their heads against Raymond's knees. Ooh-Ooh looked very grave with his drooping cheeks and bloodshot eyes, and Impikoko stretched to his full length, first on his front legs and then on his hind legs, as if to check his measurements.

"Have you grown, Impikoko?" his master said in a pampering voice. He petted them on the heads and spoke to them as if they were human.

"No, no, your master won't be naughty. Ooh-Ooh and Impikoko can stay with their master forever and ever."

He got up, stubbed out his cigar, wished the girls good night, and went to bed.

Heavy and calm, without dreams, he fell asleep.

VI.

A month passed, a month without incident, like so many others that had passed before. The Verstratjes had paid him a few more visits, and he'd been to see them, and springtime was slowly approaching, bringing high, thin skies and drowsy awakenings. The thrush was already trumpeting in the bare treetops, and the swollen blond stream babbled and sang its own melody, as it did each spring.

Everything was just the same as any other year, and yet . . . yet something had changed, not in nature, but in Raymond's mood and habits.

Before, when he went out riding, he had systematically avoided the village, regarding it as tedious and disagreeable. But for some time now, he had chosen routes that would take him straight through the village—preferably twice, on the way out and on the way home.

The Verstratjes soon figured out what he was up to, but said nothing; they grinned.

Their little procession of three always had to pass Mr. Dufour's house, where the clop of the hooves on the cobblestones summoned the sisters to the windows. The men would turn on their horses and wave. The sisters would nod and wave back with a smile. That was all. But it made a strong impression on both sides.

It was too bad for Raymond that Max was now married and gone. He had no more reason or pretext for visiting Mr. Dufour's house. He could go there anyway, if he saw no alternative, but over time, as one visit followed another, it would attract too much attention. In any case, what would he do there? How would he account for his visits? The family would soon become suspicious, and that was the last thing he wanted, because even he was far from certain what exactly he was after. All he had was the desire—and, up to a point, the need—to pass the house, to wave, and to see what happened. And what he saw, in that fast, fleeting instant, never left him unmoved; on the contrary, it drew him back time and again.

Sometimes all three of them stood at the window; other times, only two; and often just one. If one stood alone, he could count on it being Adrienne. He saw her friendly smile, the fire in her cheeks, and her eyes, beaming with emotion. That was enough for him; that filled the whole rest of his day with a captivating feeling of gentle happiness. He seemed to desire no more. He was not certain he did desire more. He sometimes felt he could have gone on that way all his life, relying on nothing else for his happiness and contentment than that fleeting wave and that smile through the window. He was sometimes afraid there *would* be more, afraid of an inner struggle that would ruin his happiness. He selfishly enjoyed what the Verstratjes, with their innuendo, had conjured up in him.

It was a good thing he never looked at the expressions on the faces of the other two sisters. They might have surprised or even shocked him. And better still that he did not hear the conversations which usually followed his fleeting appearance.

At first, the sisters were in perfect accord. The jaunty cavalcade under their windows was always a refreshing change from the stifling boredom of their everyday lives. But soon, when Edmée, and especially Clara, realized for whom these equestrian spectacles were intended, their lips began to droop and their eyes narrowed. Although they never faulted Adrienne, they began, more and more often, to disparage Raymond and his whole way of living. Adrienne would listen with burning cheeks and not say a word, but the pain she felt was sometimes cutting, and she felt her sisters were unkind and unfair in their opinion of him. Besides, it was obvious to her that they were only doing it out of a sense of jealousy, and that pained her even more. No one made a scene, but the old bond of intimacy between Adrienne and her sisters was broken.

It was like a wordless conspiracy all around Adrienne. Clara and Edmée, who had never been so very close, now seemed to have no secrets from each other; on the contrary, they were usually deep in secretive conversation, from which Adrienne was systematically excluded. When Adrienne came into the room, they would fall into sudden and conspicuous silence or begin talking of trivial matters.

This silent hostility was drawn to the surface by an unexpected visit from Max and his wife. Max had a worried look, as if preoccupied with some private concern, and after greeting Adrienne, somewhat coolly, and exchanging a few banal words with her, he arranged to take a turn in the garden with Clara and Edmée while his wife remained in the parlor with Adrienne.

There, in the back of the garden, where no one could see or hear them, the two sisters poured out all that weighed on their hearts.

"It's getting bad," said Clara. "Every two or three days he parades in front of our windows—

101

sometimes with the Verstratjes, sometimes on his own. The neighbors noticed a long time ago—how could they not?—and they laugh about it. Apparently it has even reached the ears of the Reverend Father."

"How do you know?" Max asked brusquely.

"Well . . . I believe I saw it in the way he looked at Adrienne in church last week," Clara replied, startled by this spontaneous interrogation.

Max's left hand stroked his beard, tugging it forward and pinching it into a point at the end. His eyebrows were drawn together; his eyes had a cool, hard look. He strove to give his expression a little energy. After a moment of deep, troubled thought, he spoke, like an oracle.

"If he is sincere, there can be little or no objection. But it all depends on the Aunts, of course."

"Ha! They'll hate the idea!" Clara gloated.

"Why? How do you know?!" he asked, abruptly brusque and inquisitorial again.

"Well . . . because of his bad conduct! . . . Because of the bad company he keeps! You must recall what the Aunts had to say when we visited last week," Clara said.

Again, Max solemnly stroked his beard into a thrusting point. For a moment, he thought back to the old days and all the mischief that he and Raymond had gotten up to then. His eyes turned cool and distant. That was all over now, as if it had never been. The only thing he cared about now was the future; and he looked to that distant future—not *too* distant, he hoped—with pride and eagerness. Since he had married into wealth, since he had seen and sampled the great wide world, since he had established himself as a serious member of society and soon-to-be father, new horizons of ambition had opened up to him. He planned to enter the political fray; he aimed to become a provincial councilor and perhaps a member of parliament. He had already published a couple of articles about Religion and Devotion to the Fatherland in a local paper, and before long he'd be making a speech in a political gathering. He burned with ambition, and to achieve his goal, he needed authority and support and could not have obstacles put in his way. One obstacle would be an undesirable marriage by a member of his family; one form of support would be a match of which the Aunts, with all the prestige of their considerable fortune, would approve.

He had nothing against Raymond personally; on the contrary, his old friend had wealth, power, and prestige of his own and could prove useful; but the Aunts . . . the Aunts—they pulled all the strings. Without them, he could accomplish nothing. A marriage against the will of the Aunts, with the implicit threat of later disinheritance, was simply unthinkable.

"We must wait and see how things develop," he decided at last.

"But his blatant way of courting her . . . and all the talk in town!" Clara grumbled in dissatisfaction.

"We must wait . . . wait . . ." he repeated calmly, with a consciousness of his responsibilities as the self-appointed head of the family.

"I intend to speak to Papa about it," Clara said.

"Do not do that!" he cried, almost menacingly. "Papa is much too emotional; he would ruin everything. Promise me you won't!"

With great reluctance, Clara promised she wouldn't do it yet.

They turned back toward the house, not wanting to stay away too long and rouse Adrienne's suspicion.

VII.

MAX had talked about waiting, in the interest of gaining time and of calmly and quietly watching events unfold, but when, to Clara's profound frustration, he put his foot down, he could not have suspected the wait would be so extraordinarily brief.

One afternoon, three days after Max's visit, Vreesken drove up to Mr. Dufour's house in the old coach and the three Aunts stepped stiffly out of it, while Clara, Adrienne, and Edmée, who were embroidering by the window as usual, threw aside their needlework in confusion and flew to the door. They soon realized that something very serious must be going on, for never before had the Aunts paid a visit without letting them know beforehand.

"My, my, Aunt Clemence, and Aunt Estelle, and Aunt Victoire, what a pleasure to see you so unexpectedly!" all three of them cried, in a show of utter delight. "Come in, Aunts! You're in luck, Papa is home too. He'll be so pleased to see you!"

But it seemed the nieces' rapture did not quickly or completely transfer itself to the Aunts. They had the feeling Aunt Clemence's face was especially hard and angular that afternoon, and they could very clearly hear Aunt Victoire huffing, as her eyes, looking even more spiteful than usual, darted left and right. Yet the most disturbing expression of all was on Aunt Estelle's face. Her innocent eyes were filled with a kind of trembling supplication, and she kept folding her hands together and separating them in nervous agitation.

"Where is Papa? We would very much like a word with him," asked Aunt Clemence.

As if he had heard her request, the door opened and in walked Mr. Dufour.

"*Tiens, tiens, tiens!* What's all this! *Quel bon vent vous amène?*" he cried out in surprise, mixing French with Flemish as usual.[1]

Aunt Clemence glanced suspiciously behind the door, as if in fear of committing an indiscretion. Then she repeated, with thin, hissing lips:

"We would like a word with you. Hasn't Max arrived yet?"

"Max!" they all exclaimed in great surprise.

---

1 "Well, well, well! . . . What good wind brings you here?"

"Yes, I have asked him to join us," Aunt Clemence hissed.

"Shall we leave you to your business, then?" asked Clara, who was feeling stifled. And she stood to go.

"No, absolutely not, we need everyone here," Aunt Clemence said very decidedly, knocking Clara back into her chair with a wave of her hand.

"As you wish, Aunt . . ."

"*Rien de grave?* Nothing serious, I hope?" Mr. Dufour asked, knotting his eyebrows.

Aunt Clemence offered no answer but a cold stare. He sputtered a little behind closed lips and shrugged impatiently. Aunt Estelle gave him a pleading look; Aunt Victoire huffed and narrowed her eyes. The girls didn't know what to do or what to say. Adrienne's cheeks were ablaze, and she felt tears come to her eyes without knowing why.

What a relief! . . . There was Max, riding up to the house on his bicycle! He saw the whole assembled family through the window and hurried inside.

"I beg your pardon, Aunts, for arriving so late. On my way out, I was held up by a client."

Still panting and sweating from his hasty trip, he wiped his forehead and temples with a handkerchief. After a hurried hello to his father and sisters, he took a seat.

"Can no one can hear us, or listen in?" Aunt Clemence asked in a lowered voice.

"No one," they all assured her. To guarantee their privacy, Max went to the door and locked it.

"I am here to warn you about something," Aunt Clemence began mysteriously. "Something that some of you may already have noticed or suspected . . . but that you may not yet know . . . at least, not the way we know it. Hasn't it struck you that that Mr. Raymond—you know, from Carvin—keeps riding by on horseback with his new friends—you know, the Verstratjes?"

Adrienne, who had received a brief but cutting glance from Aunt Clemence, felt the earth shift beneath her feet. The others remained as mute and still as statues, except for Mr. Dufour, who raised his eyebrows and said in a very bland tone:

"Yes, I've seen him pass by a few times, but—"

"Well, then, do you know why he passes this house so often?" Aunt Clemence asked, fixing her brother with a severe gaze.

"No . . . why should I?"

"To court one of your daughters . . . Adrienne!" Aunt Clemence said spitefully.

Adrienne smothered a cry. Everyone turned to her in consternation.

"Buh . . . buh . . . buh . . . ! How do you know?!" Mr. Dufour eventually blurted out, after turning a deep crimson.

"How we know is beside the point," Aunt Clemence hissed, "but we do know, we know it with great certainty, and that is what matters. Did *you* know?"

"Not at all . . . I didn't know the first thing about it!" Mr. Dufour confessed in all sincerity.

"Did you know, Max?"

"I, Aunt . . . I . . . all I knew is that he passed the house quite often," Max stuttered, as white as a sheet beneath his dark beard.

"Did you know, Clara, Adrienne, Edmée?"

The girls were trembling in their chairs. They stammered inarticulate answers. Adrienne was panting through her half-open mouth, as if gasping for air, and had red blotches on her face.

"Well, then, now you know," was Aunt Clemence's stern conclusion, "and so you will also know straight away what you must do—unless it should so happen," she added with a hiss, "that you are impressed with that ne'er-do-well and of a mind to welcome him to the family. That is your business; we have simply come to warn you. As far as we are concerned, we prefer to have no connection at all to the fellow."

"None whatsoever," growled Aunt Victoire.

Aunt Estelle did not say a word, but looked sad and pleading and folded her hands together. They all sat for moment in suffocating silence.

"Buh . . . buh . . . buh . . . ! Isn't this just a lot of fuss about nothing?" Mr. Dufour finally protested.

"Nothing!" Aunt Clemence sputtered. "Nothing! Only because you don't know what they're saying about it in the village and everywhere else and, I hardly need add, what slanderous lies they're telling. Your daughters' reputation is at stake! Not to mention your good name—the whole family's good name! Is that *nothing* to you?"

"But we can't prevent the lad from riding his horse past the house!" Mr. Dufour pointed out.

"No, of course not; but you *can* prevent Clara, and Edmée, and above all Adrienne, from standing in the window and giving him a friendly nod as he goes by. *That*, I should think, is entirely dispensable."

Aunt Clemence had spoken. She had said what she had come to say, and her words, so fraught with menace, hung in the stuffy air of the room where the family sat packed together. Why she felt so strongly about Raymond hardly mattered; maybe the cause lay in some dim subconscious she did not know existed; maybe she hated him for his youth, for his robust energy, for the boy-ish happiness he exuded, unlike anything ever experienced by that old maid. Be that as it may, she had spoken, and her meaning was clear to all: Adrienne and Raymond must not marry. If they did, the price would be open hostility, a family quarrel, and, in the long run, disinheritance . . .

Aunt Clemence rose from her seat.

"You're never leaving so soon! Surely you'll stay and have coffee with us!" they all cried.

Yes, they had to go; they were expecting a few ladies from their village for coffee at their house. They had just popped in to warn the family of this danger; nothing else.

They said goodbye. Not another word was spoken about the incident; enough had been said already. They were all as polite and friendly as they could be under the circumstances, and Max escorted the Aunts to their carriage and helped them in with a show of gallantry. Vreesken, huddled on the box, gave a quick farewell wave of his whip, and the old carriage rattled away.

Inside the house, a defeated silence reigned. In fact, Clara and Edmée were quite pleased with the outcome, but much less so with how it had come about. They sensed something like a personal threat: if one of them were ever to find herself in Adrienne's place . . . As for Adrienne, she had fled as soon as the Aunts were gone and was in her room, weeping. And Mr. Dufour was fuming with pent-up rage, not so much because of Raymond's unconditional rejection as a suitor, but because that rejection had been forced on him by his sisters, and he dared not oppose their tyrannical will.

Max said nothing. He sat gazing into the distance, pale and grave, absorbed in a deep interior study of the situation. He was tensely calculating the potential costs and benefits to his future career. But whatever the outcome, the important thing for now was not to delay, but to obey.

He abruptly stood, stroked his beard out into a point, wrinkled his face into grave solemnity, and said to Clara and Edmée, in a firm, almost chiding tone:

"So, no matter what, do not stand in the window ever again when he rides past!"

Clara felt a burst of defiance. "We don't need that kind of accusation from you!" she exclaimed with feeling.

"I say what I say," he pontificated, staring at her coolly.

To Clara, his tone was unbearable. She marched out of the room, slamming the door behind her. Edmée pouted and turned her back on him.

"Buh . . . buh . . . buh . . ." grumbled Mr. Dufour, put out.

VIII.

TWO days later, when Raymond came parading past Mr. Dufour's house with the Verstratjes, he could not spy a single living creature through the front windows. Baffled, he checked the sides of the house and the upper floor but found no one. He told himself the girls must have gone out; he would see them on his way back. But when he returned, the house seemed as lifeless as ever, and Raymond was deeply disappointed; the Verstratjes, who could see his frustration, chuckled under their breath.

The very next morning he was back, this time unaccompanied. Once more, not a living creature by the windows. Raymond was mystified. He went for a long ride, came back, and again saw no one. He had the feeling a few of the Dufours' neighbors were sneering at him as he passed. When two days later he came by again, and again spied no one, he understood that something must have happened. But what? How could he find out? He had no pretext at all for visiting the Dufour family. It would look very odd if he did. If Max were still living there, then of course! Hang on . . . . Max! What if he paid a visit to Max? He really should have done it long ago! He owed him a visit; since his friend's marriage, he hadn't visited once. He was sure to learn something that way, if there was anything to be learned.

One afternoon, after some hesitation, he had Jan hitch up his dogcart and drive him to the small, neighboring town where Max now lived.

It was a fine, cool, sunny day in early spring. Nothing had yet turned green except the meadows, but there was a mildness in the air, and the thrushes and blackbirds sang as if it were the height of summer. The cart rattled down a canalside path of gravel golden with sunshine, and Impikoko ran alongside it, elated, his pink tongue dangle-panting from his mouth.

He wanted to know; he needed to know! His feelings for Adrienne, stoked by adversity, had grown firmer and stronger. It was clearer to him now what he wanted; he was roused to battle. Love had awakened inside him, true love!

In the distance, he soon saw the town's towers and factory chimneys; he crossed a drawbridge with creaky hinges; he entered a long, broad street.

He knew the number: 72. The even numbers were on the right, and he passed the houses slowly, keeping track: 58, 60, 62, 64 . . . A side street, two houses without visible numbers, and then suddenly 72, a banal new building made of bright white stone, with a copper plate on the heavy oak door . . . he had arrived!

He leapt out of the cart and rang the door-bell.

"Is the man of the house in?" he asked the maid who opened the door. But he didn't have to wait for an answer: Max himself was just coming into the hall and saw Raymond at his doorstep.

"*Bonjour*, Max, I've come to see you!" he cried.

"Come in, come in . . ." said Max, coming up to him and extending his hand with a sheepish smile and something like hesitation.

This cool reception was not lost on Raymond.

"Is this a bad time?" he asked hesitantly.

"No, no, I can spare a moment," Max replied, with what seemed like effort, and he pushed a door open.

They were standing in a salon where the heavy curtains admitted a dreary half-light. The room was furnished in a busy style, with too much red velvet and copper on the chairs and tables and too much gilt adorning the frames on the walls.

Raymond glanced at the huge portrait of the Pope hung opposite the portraits of Marie and Max in their wedding finery. On an étagère, among jars and vases, were smaller photos of all the rest of the family.

"Have a seat! Would you like a glass of wine?" Max asked.

"*Non, merci!*" Raymond replied. "I never drink in the afternoon. I've come to see the new home you've made for yourself and find out how you're doing."

"Very well, thank you," Max said dryly.

"And Marie?"

"The same!"

Silence followed. They looked into each other's eyes and felt the pressure of what they were keeping from each other. Max's expression was cool, severe, and grave. He tugged his beard into a point and looked out through one of the windows into the street.

"And back at home! . . . How are things there?" Raymond eventually asked.

"At my father's house?" said Max.

"Yes."

"Just fine, as far as I know, but . . ." He trailed off and fixed his former friend with a solemn look.

"But . . . ?" Raymond repeated nervously.

116

"Well," Max said, "there is one thing . . . To be honest, I'm glad you stopped by, because I've been meaning to talk to you about it."

"What is it?" Raymond asked.

"Don't take this the wrong way," Max said, "but it's with regard to you riding past the house, with the Verstratjes."

"How so?"

"Well . . . the neighbors have noticed you passing by so often, and people will talk. The Aunts caught wind of it, and . . . eh, you do understand, don't you?"

Raymond understood . . . All at once he understood only too well . . . It was now as clear as day why he hadn't seen Adrienne at the window anymore. The Aunts detested him—that much had been obvious at the wedding party—and they had put their veto on the match. He had no need to hear anything more; he knew and understood everything. Nervously, he rose and held out his hand to Max.

"Forgive me," he said. "Please . . . please accept my apologies."

"No apologies necessary," said Max. "Only . . . as a favor to me, you might . . . ride by there a little less often, past the windows, because of the gossip . . . You do understand?"

"Never fear," Raymond said in a resolute tone, "they won't see me there again. *Adieu . . . adieu.*"

"Still friends, I hope?" said Max, showing him the door.

"Of course! Of course. What reason does either of us have to be offended? My best regards to Marie," he added hurriedly.

And he hopped into his cart and was gone.

His first feeling, as he filled his lungs with the free air, was a wondrous calm. A calm of liberation, of release, such as a person must feel who has escaped deadly peril without a scratch. Within him rose a cheer of jubilation, as though, instead of scorn, he had received a tribute. Only some time later did he realize that these feelings issued from his wounded pride. So . . . the Aunts didn't think he was good enough for one of their nieces! Very well, then, their niece would see no more of him. What luck . . . what incredible luck that he had never made any real advances! Riding past her windows on horseback—what did that amount to? It was everyone's right to ride there. Could you call that a declaration of love? Or a formal proposal of marriage? He let out a wholehearted laugh at the very notion; he laughed out loud in his carriage, startling Jan, who looked back in surprise, with a flush, and then broke into quiet chuckling of his own.

"Ah do believe ye laughed, sir," said the man-servant in a diffident voice.

"Right ye are, Jan! Ah laughed," Raymond answered, a little disturbed himself by his unguarded outburst of amusement. "Laughin's better than weepin', now, isna it?" he added as a sort of apology.

"Ha! Tha's for sure, sir!" Jan agreed.

As soon as they were back at Carvin, Raymond went to the kitchen and said to Manse, "Manse, I'm hungry this evenin'. 'Appen y'ave owt to eat here?"

"Shall y'ave gutbreads?" Manse asked, her eyes glittering.

"Y'ave gutbreads in th'ouse?" he exclaimed.

"Ah 'ave! Throatbreads, an' good'uns at that!" she boasted. "'Ow would ye like 'em? Fried, wi' young peas? But they're outer a box . . . !"

"Goo on! Throatbreads outer a box!" he teased.

"Gi' o'er, ye spunky devil!" she cough-laughed, poking him with her elbow. "Ah mean th'peas! But they're so good an' fresh!"

"Bring 'em on, then!" he laughed, in good spirits.

He ate his "gutbreads" with gusto, washing them down with three-quarters of a bottle of his finest Burgundy.

"Will y'ave a plate of hare pâté as well?" Manse asked from the open door to the kitchen.

"Ah'll say! Let's 'ave it!"

He ate two slices of pâté and finished his bottle. Well-fed and a little dizzy, he stretched out in his armchair in front of the fire with a good cigar.

"The Aunts! . . . The Aunts! . . ." he chortled to himself.

He opened the paper but could not understand what he was reading. What was the use of knowing what was in the paper, anyway? He closed his eyes and gradually dozed off.

He dreamed and had strange visions. It was as though he heard sorrowful wailing and saw creatures all around him weeping in agony. They were women, mostly one woman, but whatever he did, he could neither glimpse her face nor recognize her.

He seemed to know who she was but could not think of her name. He turned toward her; he spoke to her, pleading and soon weeping with her, but she kept turning away and hiding her sobbing face in her trembling hands. He wanted to follow her, and she forbade him. He called her to him, and she refused to come. She was the very image of Sorrow and Agony—helpless sorrow, capable only of suffering.

He woke with a violent start. His bewildered eyes scanned all around for the harrowing scene from his nightmare. He saw nothing but the ordinary, familiar objects that surrounded him every day, but outside, in the night, he heard something like a long, plaintive moan, as someone, framed in the doorway to the kitchen, seemed to burst into a fit of squawking laughter.

"Manse! What's up wi' ye?" he cried in confusion.

"It's ah as should be askin' what's up wi' *ye!*" Manse laughed. "Blartin' an' gosterin' like that! Ye mun've dreamed aloud, ah s'pose?"

He sat up straight with a disoriented look and listened with fear in his eyes to the howling, outside, in the night.

"What *is* that?" he asked.

"Canna hear it's th'gale?" Manse said mockingly. "Ye're 'alf-asleep yet, ah do believe!"

"Th'gale!" he said. "Since when? What time is it?"

"Near ten o'clock! Ah was abaht ter wake ye. 'tis time for bed."

Upstairs, in his room, he heard it even more clearly: the rising howl of the wind. It must have started while he was napping by the fire, and now he understood the weeping and wailing in his dream. It was the wind coming up, its near-human voices racing and howling through the house.

He pushed one of his windows open and stared out into the night. The wind was rounding the corner of the house from the southwest, making the bare treetops hiss and shiver. It came rumbling from afar—very, very far, from the gloomy, hollow depths of the night—to batter Carvin's pale walls with brute force, and seemed to chase the moon savagely out before it among torn scraps of cloud. The water sloshed in the moat with a hollow sound, as if slopping back and forth in an echoing cellar.

As Raymond stood staring, his thoughts turned to the events of the day. And for the first time, he was struck, deep within, by the vivid image of the woman who had set off the whole chain of events. How could he not have thought of Adrienne until now?! How could he not have paused to wonder how the unexpected blow had affected her? If he loved her at all, how could he never have thought for an instant of *her* sorrow and *her* suffering, instead feeling only the sting of the humiliation visited on him by the Aunts? . . . Well, she was now in his innermost thoughts, and his heart ached with remorse and self-reproach. He sensed what she must be suffering, sensed that she had nothing to console her, no one to offer encouragement or support. What would become of her and him? Was that over now, over and done forever? Would they never see each other again, never even exchange an innocent greeting or a smile? . . . In the stormy night, he thought of her, and his wayward emotions flew to her, as it were, on the wings of the wind. The complaints and the sobs he had heard in his dream were hers and his, two souls howling to each other for help, roughly and ruthlessly pulled apart, longing, needing to find each other again. They had to . . . they had to . . . ! This was not the final chapter, not the end. It was not up to strangers, but to him and her, to know what they wanted, to know how to lead their lives!

His staring eyes grew hard and stern with willpower; his lips quivered. He would have it . . . he wanted it! It was his right, his duty. He felt a wayward growl within like the growling gale of that stormy night; the forces unleashed could never be rechained.

He had made his decision. He wanted to find out, he would find out! He couldn't see her any more, but he could find a way to have a letter delivered to her. He would write to her!

He closed the shutter with a bang and sat down at his writing desk. He wrote and wrote . . . It was his soul that supplied the feelings and dictated his words. He acted without the least hesitation; he could not do otherwise.

The night in no way altered his firm resolve. The next morning, he reread what he had written and could not see any way to improve it. He asked to speak to her alone—somewhere, anywhere. He did not want to send the letter by mail; it might fall into the wrong hands. After long hesitation, weighing his options, he bought, for a very modest fee, the "eternal silence" of Floorke, Mr. Dufour's coachman. At the first favorable opportunity, Floorke was to deliver the letter to Adrienne, in strictest confidence.

A week went by before Floorke, one evening at sundown, came to Raymond with the reply. It was brief: just a few lines, in a shaky hand. But such love and suffering as those few lines expressed!

She loved him . . . loved him . . . more than words could say, but dared not . . . no . . . she dared not come to him in secret. She begged him not to write to her again and not to try to see her anymore, but to wait . . . to wait a while, in the hope of better times. She would remain faithful to him, and never, ever, forget him—that much he could count on.

With a heavy sigh, as if relieved, Raymond slid the letter into his pocket. How was he feeling now? Was he disappointed, or was he contented? He felt at peace, a great, deep, sudden peace. She loved him and knew that he returned her feelings; that was a milestone, a beacon, a certainty. Wait . . . yes, he would wait. The day before, he had felt nervous and rushed; now all at once he felt calm inside; he could wait . . .

It was a mild, quiet evening, with delicate oranges and pinks and grays low in the west. The birds sung in the garden; the first leaves were budding; love and promise hung in the air.

Yes, he would wait . . . he would wait.

IX.

SO spring came, and summer. Life went on in quiet monotony. Mr. Dufour had the usual business affairs of a man of leisure, which did not demand much of his energy; the girls sat by the windows with their embroidery and went to church twice a day; and the thing that had so upset them all was never mentioned. Adrienne kept her secret buried in the depths of her soul and cherished dreams for the future; Raymond was no longer spotted riding his horse past their windows.

What was he doing? What had become of him? She had no idea: he was faithful to her wishes.

In the late summer Marie gave birth to a son. It was a delight and a stroke a good fortune, just what both of them had so ardently wished! Everything had gone so well and so smoothly, and

Max himself rode over on his bicycle to tell them the good news. They were all in a happy, excited state and asked who the godparents would be and under what name the child would be baptized.

"I'm here to ask you to be the godfather, Papa," Max replied.

"Why, of course!" said Mr. Dufour, who was overcome for a moment and choked back tears. "And the godmother . . . ?"

"Aunt Clemence. I hope she will say yes. I have to make the offer, at least. I'll ride over there next."

They all nodded in unconditional approval. That was just as it should be. "And the name . . . the name?" they asked impatiently.

Max scratched his head, and his face stretched into a grimace.

"On that count, Marie and I do not quite see eye to eye," he said. "She was determined to call him Sylvain, a favorite name of hers. I eventually made her realize that was impossible—that out of respect for Aunt Clemence, we must use Aunt's name. In other words, Clement," Max said with a smile, "and the second name is Papa's, Louis, and the third, to make Marie happy, is Sylvain. Clement Louis Sylvain Dufour. That doesn't sound half bad."

They were all in complete agreement about that. Mr. Dufour, very touched, gave a husky cough and rubbed his eyes. The girls were aflutter with excitement and tender feelings and insisted on visiting the mother and child without delay. They had Mr. Dufour ask Floorke to harness the horses to the landau, while Max rode on to the Aunts' house as fast as he could.

Aunt Clemence was genuinely surprised and gratified and agreed with immediate enthusiasm. Her hard features blossomed into a smile that looked grossly out of place and somewhat resembled a grimace. Aunt Estelle clapped her hands in excitement, and even Aunt Victoire sniggered in quiet approval. They offered Max a glass of port and produced a humidor of cigars, an unprecedented event. Max had never guessed that they owned such a thing and, grinning with pleasure, expressed his surprise.

"It's for the Reverend Father when he visits." Aunt Clemence's voice was solemn, almost devout.

As they nipped at their port, they asked after Adrienne. Was she still at all attached to that gentleman . . . you know, that . . . Raymond, at Carvin.

128

"Absolutely not . . . that's all over and forgotten," Max reassured them.

"Thank goodness," said Aunt Clemence in a haughty tone. Aunt Estelle folded her hands together and looked around with pining eyes; Aunt Victoire huffed and shot spiteful looks in all directions.

He was given a second glass of port and, on the way out, invited to slip a few cigars in his pocket.

"And your political career, how is that going?" asked Aunt Clemence.

"Very well, Aunt. I believe in October I'll be elected to the provincial council."

Aunt Clemence nodded gravely.

"It would bring great honor to the family," she remarked.

"It may also be a stepping stone to greater things," he replied, with false humility.

All three nodded gravely in agreement.

In the life of the village, the baptism was an exceptional event. All three Aunts were in attendance, and Aunt Clemence held her godchild over the font as if carrying the child of God Himself in her arms. Aunt Estelle wept. Aunt Clemence gave her a strict, admonishing look, but Estelle couldn't help herself; her emotions overwhelmed her. Aunt Victoire was on her best behavior, except for a sort of revolted grin when the tiny thing started to cry. Mr. Dufour stood by awkwardly, uncertain what to do with himself. The three nieces, deeply moved, sat motionless some distance away, their eyes wide.

The party at Max's house was a touching affair. Marie had already made such a good recovery that she could receive not only the family, but also a few intimate acquaintances, who ringed the bed where she lay with a beatific smile on her face and her child at her side. The little tot was admired, comparisons were drawn to other family members, and now and then Marie pressed him gently to her chest and kissed him with the intimacy known only to a mother. Then the Aunts and nieces stood by like strangers. For an instant, a chasm opened, as it were, between the young mother and those other, dried-up women. And the men too felt out of place there, and stood for a moment like intruders, as if they'd committed some indistinct crime. The sacred aura of motherhood prevailed . . . Only the mother and child existed; everything else was happenstance, mere incident.

They did not stay long; Marie needed her rest. Max led them quietly out of the room and there, on a side table, were beautiful boxes of bonbons and sweets, a gift to the lady visitors from Aunt Clemence's generous purse. It was a day of pure joy and happiness, full of harmony and of mild, moving scenes.

X.

THE last sheaves of oats rose like grayish-yellow dwarves from the new-shorn stubble fields. The days were becoming shorter, and the sweet summer birds had flown. Autumn was on the advance, with gold in the treetops and evening skies of apotheosis in the west.

At Carvin, Raymond had spent his summer in anticipation. Anticipation of what? He himself wasn't sure. But anticipation it was . . .

He had bowed to Adrienne's express wishes. He had not written to her again, had no longer tried to see her.

Yet he had seen her. He saw her every Sunday at Mass. He sat some distance away from her, in a place from which he could see her clearly, and from there he exchanged meaningful looks with her. That was enough. Those looks said everything. They sent him home fortified, until the following Sunday.

That went on all summer long. He kept himself busy, going on frequent rides with the Verstratjes, and barely noticed the weeks flitting by. But now that winter was approaching, now that the days were becoming shorter and the evenings longer, he sometimes sat pondering and daydreaming and felt the loneliness of his life.

Waiting . . . how much longer? Would he have to go on waiting all the long winter? . . . And winter would give way to spring and summer and so on . . . . How long? . . . How long? . . . A rising impatience gripped his nerves, irritating and agitating him; in that condition, he could see no way out of the impasse.

Why go on waiting any longer . . . and what for? For the Aunts to have a change of heart? . . . For the Aunts to die! But those tough old biddies, who hated him all the more because they had no real motive to hate him, would never change their minds and might still have long years ahead of them; to wait for that would be an absurd self-deception.

What did he care, and what use did he have for whatever fortune they might possess? His own income was more than adequate; he could marry whenever, and whomever, he liked.

He had to put an end to this. He had waited long enough and was ready to defy the will of the

Aunts. He could no longer stand the thought that those three old dragons had, in a manner of speaking, taken charge of his life and overruled his free will. Each day, the humiliation felt more unbearable; it struck at the heart of his self-respect, and he decided he would no longer defer to Adrienne's wishes. He wrote to tell her they could not go on this way—he wanted, he needed to see and speak to her. He was precise and categorical, stating a place and time for their meeting. "The day after tomorrow, at the stroke of seven in the evening," he wrote to her, "I shall wait for you in the back of your garden, where the path winds closest to the hedge. I have no doubt you can come to me at that hour if you choose, even if only for a few minutes. I must see you and have a word with you. I cannot and do not wish to go on living this way. I beg you, come to me, if only as briefly as a flash of lightning. If you are not there the day after tomorrow, I shall return the following day at the same time, and so on and so forth, until I finally see you. So come to me! Come!"

On the appointed day, shortly before the appointed hour, he arrived in the place he had described. The early evening was dark and silent, unlit by the moon or stars. The lonely country road ran along the backs of the gardens and the houses; there were a few bushes behind which he could hide if he had to. The air, a little chilly, threatened rain.

He heard the seven hard, slow strokes fall from the church tower like the hammer of fate. His eyes opened wide, and through a gap in the hedge he stared into the darkness, pricking his ears for the slightest noise.

He stood and waited, running his fingers over the leafless twigs of the hedge, which were cold and clammy. His eyes, gradually adjusting to the dark, made out vaguely, behind a bush, the pale path through Mr. Dufour's garden. He tried to calm his breath; blood rushed to his temples; he felt and even seemed to hear his heart hammering.

He stood like that, motionless, for a few minutes. Would she come? Or not? The great tempest of emotion slowly subsided. He did not think she would come. He understood now that what had seemed so easy and natural to him was too risky for her. Maybe it was all for the best that she hadn't come. The risk was too great. He had decided she would not come and was already turning to go, his senses quieted, when he heard a vague and hasty rustling. The rustling came to a sudden stop, and a dark silhouette stood before him, on the other side of the hedge.

"Adrienne!" he called out in a husky voice. And without thinking, he burst through the hedge, ran up to her, and took her in his arms.

"Let go of me! Let go of me! I have to go." Her voice was pinched; she gasped for breath.

"Adrienne!" he groaned with passion, "Adrienne! Adrienne!" And crushing her close to him as if to break her, he pressed wild kisses on her mouth and cheeks.

"Let me go! I have to go!" she repeated, suffocating.

"You've only just arrived! Stay for one minute . . . one second!" he moaned.

"I can't, I don't dare, they'd come looking for me."

"Then at least tell me when I may come back?"

"I don't know! Go away! Go away! I don't dare!"

"I'll come back tomorrow!" he cried, letting go of her.

"You mustn't!"

"The day after tomorrow?"

"You mustn't!"

"I must! I shall! I'll write to you!"

She was already gone.

"Adrienne! . . ." he called after her.

Panting for air, she stopped.

"Do you love me?"

"Oh . . . !" was all he heard. The next moment she melted into the night and was gone.

He stood there a long while, utterly motion-less, as if he expected she might yet return. He felt so strange inside, so strangely quiet all of a sudden. It was as if, wide awake, he were dreaming . . . Had she really been there at all . . . or had it been only an illusion? . . . And why had she fled so abruptly, as if to escape assault by a criminal? What use did he have for a meeting like that . . . an infernal torment!

He ran his hand over his forehead, as if to dispel a dark vision. All his passion had ebbed; he stood there as soberly as a mischievous boy who knows he's gone too far. Standing there now, he felt ashamed of himself, ashamed at the thought that someone might see him there, and he slipped away through the hedge like a thief and carefully closed the parted branches behind him. He could not breathe freely until he reached the ordinary paved road where all may walk.

XI.

HE resented Adrienne's fearful, overhasty flight but had no inkling of what she had gone through before she could bring herself to meet with him.

In the full freedom of his own life, he could not imagine the inner struggle of a young girl raised under all sorts of pressure and prejudice. He could not suspect what an enormous step it had been for her to defy all her deep-seated principles and respond to his summons. When she looked back with a calm, clear mind, she felt she had behaved like a girl of the pavement; her maid Martha, she was certain, would never have taken such a risk.

Ten times, a hundred times, she had cast aside the idea with all her strength, resolving to herself, *I will not go.* Yet her love was too strong; she had succumbed; and now she counted it against herself as a scandalous crime, a betrayal of her father and of her whole family.

She lay thinking about it and trembling in her bed and felt a kind of disgust with herself. His wild kisses were still burning on her lips and she did not know what was more overwhelming: the dizzying passion of the pleasure she had tasted, or the horror of having tasted it. If at that instant her father or sisters had come to her bedside and asked her what she had done, she would have admitted to everything, accepted their well-deserved contempt with humility and something like joy, and submitted to harsh punishments. In the excessive propriety of her naive conscience, she felt lost, morally and almost physically, and in her bewilderment, she could see no other way out than the confessional, than unconditional submission and a full declaration of guilt to her confidential father confessor.

She lay brooding over it all night, and by the time the first hint of day lit the edge of her curtains, she had made her decision.

She rose, dressed hurriedly, and tiptoed downstairs. Martha was already lighting a fire in the kitchen and looked up, startled and almost alarmed by Adrienne's untimely entrance. But when Adrienne simply told her she wished to go to confession, she took it as very natural. The girls often went to confession without prior notice.

When one of them feared she had sinned, whether in word or act, they would sometimes set out early in the morning to consult her confessor.

Adrienne hurried, fearing she would be too late. Thank goodness, she was still in time. When she arrived in the chilly, twilit church, where only a few small lamps shed a wistful light, her eye fell straight away on the three women in black hooded capes seated by the confessional. She joined the row and waited. She folded her hands together and prayed with heartfelt devotion, bowing her head low. A woman came out of the confessional; another took her place; Adrienne slid over.

Then it was her turn. With faltering steps, she went up the stairs and kneeled on the hard bench. The latticed screen was shut. The Reverend Father was hearing the confession of another penitent on the other side. That went on for quite some time. Adrienne felt her cheeks burning and her temples pounding. Finally, the screen opened.

Through the lattice, Adrienne saw the Reverend Father in his pleated white surplice. His eyes were closed, his hands folded together. He was praying. A delicate white linen handkerchief lay spread across his heavy chest.

He opened his eyes and looked at her with an expression both gentle and grave.

❋

He listened, leaning in toward the screen, his white hand shielding his eyes. He let her speak without interruption, but once in a while a sigh escaped him and his shoulders made a motion—as if, now and then, her confession shocked every fiber of his being. When she reached the end, he slowly removed his hand from his eyes, looked at her gently and gravely, and whispered, "You have committed a great sin. I can absolve you only if you feel deep remorse and have the firm intention not to fall into sin again."

"I feel remorse, and I promise," she said with a sob.

He did not ask her who the seducer was. Maybe he knew or guessed, but he had no need to know. He spoke to her of her duties and of the wickedness of her deception. Then he folded his hands together again, closed his eyes, and immersed himself in a long prayer. Adrienne was weeping in silence. It was as if something inside her had snapped. He looked up and seeing, with a sort of flinch, her tears, he spoke quiet words of consolation. She had to pray and hope, he told her. All could be made right again; our dear Lord would take pity upon her.

For the third time, he closed his eyes, folded his hands, and murmured a few Latin words. Though she could not guess their meaning, their warm reassurance washed over her. He imposed a penance, made a quick little cross, and gently slid the screen shut. With her head deeply bowed, she rose to her feet and returned to her chair.

XII.

RAYMOND was one of those people who lead light and easy lives and are unaccustomed to struggle or opposition. He was not by any means stupid; he had practical intelligence and usually asked no more or better of life than what was well within his power to attain. But when a thing he considered attainable was withheld from him by misfortune or defiance, it awoke a sudden determination and fighting spirit that one would never have imagined him to possess. An unruly horse was a horse he would go to any lengths to tame through tenacity and patience; a dog that refused to obey was a dog he would teach the meaning of obedience. He was never rough, but persistent, with all the force of his strength and robust health. When he reached the point of wanting something, he had to have it.

He wanted Adrienne and had to have her! . . . The love sown in him by the Verstratjes with their casual innuendo, the love that might have withered as spontaneously as it had flourished, had now, through opposition and struggle, become to him a matter of life and death. He had set his sights on it; he was no longer willing to let go. He longed for Adrienne, he wanted her, but just as much, or maybe more, he wanted to break the opposition of the Aunts and anyone else who stood in his way.

He sent her another letter proposing a second rendezvous, in the same place and at the same hour. He received a reply: she would not come. She begged him not to insist, she wrote that she could not, she did not dare, her conscience forbade it. She did not tell him she had gone to confession with the Reverend Father.

He gritted his teeth and went to the rendezvous anyway. She did not come; he'd known she wouldn't come; but the next day he let her know that he had been there, and that he would go back the next day, and keep going back until he finally saw her.

She replied that he must not have any idea of the terrible suffering he was causing her. "Won't you wait? Can't you be patient?" she pleaded. "You're torturing me. You're killing me."

"You don't love me!" he accused her. "You have never loved me, and that will be the ruin of both of us. If you truly loved me, what would you care about the Aunts, or anyone or anything else? Let them keep their money; after all, I have enough for us both. Dare to be happy, won't you? Dare to live, can't you? If you truly care about me, as you claim, then no force in the world can keep us apart.

"I shall return tonight!" he concluded, "And tomorrow, and the next day, until I finally see you again and press you in my arms."

Then, one evening, she finally came to him! He heard a wild rustling of dry leaves underfoot, and the next moment she stood before him, a black silhouette in the darkening evening, bathed in the feeble glow of the pale moonlight. He broke through the hedge and wrapped her in his arms. She offered no resistance and no longer attempted, as she had at first, to wrestle free of his grasp. Her head sank to his chest, and thus they remained a long while, without speaking a word. He pressed her to him and felt her body, weaker, thinner.

"Adrienne, you've grown thin," he finally sighed.

"Yes . . ." she whispered, and they were silent again, in that tight embrace.

Something sad stole over him, like heartfelt compassion.

"Are you sick?" he asked softly.

"I've suffered so," she sighed.

He let go of her and examined her in the vague moonlight. He saw her pale face, her hollow cheeks, and her sunken eyes.

"Oh!" he cried in dismay.

"I couldn't go on . . . I couldn't go on . . ." she moaned. He stared in silence.

"I harassed you . . . forced you . . . forgive me," he said, after some time, with a choked sob.

"I forgive you."

"Go now," he said softly, almost frightened to realize that she was no longer begging him to release her.

"Will it be enough for you this time?" she asked, with a pained smile.

"I . . . I adore you," he sighed, "but I don't dare ask you to return again. I shall go back to waiting . . . I'll wait."

"How kind you are . . . so kind and sweet," she sighed, and without warning she burst into tears.

He crushed her passionately in his arms again and covered her face with kisses.

"It's good . . . oh, it's so good and soft," she whispered, in a rapture of surrender.

"May I write to you again?" he asked, letting go of her.

"Yes . . . yes . . ."

"But not come again?" he pleaded.

"Not now . . . not now . . . wait . . . for now, wait."

He fell to his knees before her and folded his hands in a gesture of adoration.

"Go now," he said, "go now . . ."

"Stand up," she begged him.

"In a moment, once you've gone. Now go . . ."

She left. He saw her dark silhouette disappear behind the bushes and scrambled to his feet.

He crept through the hedge, closed the gap behind him, and rushed off.

XIII.

ONCE again, the radiant gates of spring opened wide . . . and the world breathed new life!

The sunny days had become much too long for lovers to meet at dusk unnoticed; all Adrienne and Raymond had left was their secret correspondence, which Floorke faithfully delivered.

Their forced separation was not a source of suffering. There was something new in their love for one another, something calm and strong. They told each other in their letters what they could not say in words; between them a bond had been forged, as strong as eternity, never to be broken.

They had decided to wait, and they waited . . . but they would not wait forever. They had settled on a date: the beginning of winter. If nothing changed before that time—that is to say, if there was still no hope that the family and the Aunts would approve of their match—then they would bring matters to a head. They would elope—she would run off with him!

What inner struggle had led her to this decision? She herself hardly knew. It had welled up from within like an irrepressible force of nature. She had thrown everything overboard; in the blink of an eye, she had changed utterly, made a complete turnaround, after those days of unbearable inner torment, which had ended the evening she finally submitted and fell into his arms. Even the Reverend Father's ominous warnings no longer had any hold on her; she no longer went to confession with him; she no longer found any consolation in the idea that he could lead her back to the fold.

She saw Raymond from a distance now and then, but without ever having the chance to speak a word to him. He began to ride through the village again, on his own or with the Verstratjes, but not often, and since she always knew from his letters when he would be coming, he made sure she could always see him and exchange a quick glance with him. He also went to Mass every Sunday, where he could look at her longer, unnoticed and undisturbed.

She seemed to be in much better form . . . and yet . . . yet something about her was different than it had been, something that was strange to him and somehow disturbing. It was in the look with which her eyes met his. Before, when he had looked at her, she had always lowered her eyes and blushed. Now she no longer did. Now she looked back at him and kept looking, so strangely, so staringly, and sometimes with such a defiant, half-wild expression, that more than once it was he who lowered his eyes, abashed. It made him uneasy, even frightened, he couldn't help it, and every time he shook off the image, it forced itself on him again; her look sometimes reminded him of his cows' gleaming eyes when they were rutting and scented a nearby bull. It sent a shiver through him, followed by a great surge of love and compassion. In her eyes, he read the passionate glow of what she had promised him, and his whole being harnessed itself to achieve that happiness for them both.

XIV.

IN the course of that summer, three momentous events took place. In May, after a hard-fought campaign, Max was elected to the provincial legislature. In July, Aunt Victoire came down with a sudden and unexpected illness, and her recovery was difficult. And by late September, Marie was expecting her second child!

Max's success was triumphantly celebrated. Mr. Dufour, beaming with paternal pride, gave a banquet in his honor, with the Aunts among the guests, and predicted that in less than two years' time, his son would be a member of the Lower House of Parliament.

Max made a show of humility, acknowledging what an honor his election was, but adding that he saw it, above all, as a duty and a responsibility laid on his shoulders, a test that would call on him to prove his mettle before he could even think of moving on to the higher office that his father so prematurely envisaged for him. All this he expressed in long, elegant sentences of the kind he used when he spoke at political gatherings, in his eyes the solemn, superior look of a future minister, all the while stroking his beard into a thrusting point, that repeated gesture, now an ingrained habit, which seemed an unmistakable sign of a firm, fixed assurance that all the prerequisites of that high office were indeed in his possession. The delighted Aunts treated him as if he were already a very great man, and the sisters looked up at him with timid admiration and perhaps lost the nerve to rebel against his authoritarian dictates, as Clara, in particular, had now and then dared to do.

It was not long afterwards that Aunt Victoire had a sudden and severe attack of flu, which hit her so hard she was soon at death's door. This shook the family to its foundations. Max, in particular, who was really beginning to think of himself as the head of the family, rode his bicycle to the Aunts' country house almost every day. There he had long confidential conversations with the doctor and also, with some frequency, ran into the village priest, whose visits were proliferating at a pace that neither especially pleased nor reassured Max. The Reverend Father was always very polite and solemn toward Max, addressing him in French and calling him "Monsieur le Conseiller" at every opportunity, but all these polite, friendly gestures were the very thing that aroused Max's suspicions. He sensed a very dangerous rival on the prowl for his wealthy Aunt's fortune and was constantly on guard whenever he visited.

All the commotion surrounding Aunt Victoire appeared to escape her entirely. She took hardly any notice of what happened; she was in a deep depression. She had removed her false teeth, and her wrinkled face had collapsed completely. She no longer looked like herself. Only her eyes lived on, as spiteful as ever, observing the world in silence. Aunt Estelle spent most of her time at the bedside in tears; Aunt Clemence paced through the house, agitated and active. Aunt Victoire eventually recovered halfway, but her appetite never returned, and her jawbones seemed to have shrunk: her false teeth no longer fit. She put them away in a drawer, next to her jewelry.

But the most momentous occurrence of all, by far, was the news that Marie might for the second time become a mother.

They had kept it secret for as long as possible—no one understood why, exactly—and it was hardly visible from the outside, but in the end, they had no choice but to tell the Aunts. Max went to his father's house one afternoon to make the announcement, with grave self-confidence and the confiding, nebulous smile of an able diplomat

153

disclosing a momentous state secret. The shock was too much for the sisters; they were thunderstruck, as it were, by this bolt from the blue; only Adrienne, in her overexcitement, let out a sudden cheer:

"Oh! Wonderful! Wonderful! When is it due?"

"Adrienne!" Clara cried out, scandalized, as if her sister had said something improper. Edmée, too, peered at her sister in disapproval and curled her lower lip.

"Probably in late September," Max replied, with a superior air, as if he had not noticed the impact of his words.

As he had predicted, Marie gave birth on one of the final days of September—this time to a girl. A boy and a girl: a family fit for a king, and they all rejoiced! Max had the power, it seemed, to shape the events of life to his will and wishes. Mr. Dufour was moved to tears again, and the sisters said, "I suppose you'll baptize this one under the name of Mathilde, as Marie was hoping?"

Max gazed coolly into the distance and stroked his beard into a point. He had other plans. The elderly aunt with whom Marie had lived for so many years had been named Mathilde, and it was Marie's fervent wish, as an expression of piety and grateful memory, to give her child that name. But Max had made her see that the more vital thing was not to neglect the Aunts, *his* Aunts.

"What?! Aunt Estelle this time?" Marie cried in protest. "Aunt Estelle is a good, sweet woman, but I've always felt that her first name is ugly and horrid!"

Max remained calm.

"Not only Aunt Estelle, but also Aunt Victoire," he explained.

"How so?" Marie asked.

"Well . . . Estelle . . . Victoire . . . and a couple of other names if you like. You know . . . Aunt Victoire doesn't have long to live. We should be capable of at least this gesture. And we can't forget Aunt Estelle entirely, can we?"

Marie wept bitterly.

"And I would so much have liked to honor the memory of my dear Aunt Mathilde," she wailed.

"Next time . . . I promise," he said solemnly.

She looked at him in astonishment. "What do you mean, next time?! You expect me simply to go on . . . !" she cried in anger.

"Settle down, little woman, settle down. It's not good for you to overexcite yourself," he said soothingly, and he gave her a kiss.

And everything went as he had decided it would.

He visited the Aunts to seek their approval of the plan to baptize the child Estelle-Victoire. Aunt Estelle wept with grateful emotion, and even

Aunt Victoire gave signs of satisfaction, although she moaned that her poor health would prevent her from attending the ceremony.

"Oh, then I won't go either. I'll stay here with you," said kindly Aunt Estelle without a moment's thought.

Max affected deep regret but added that of course he understood; and the child was baptized without the Aunts.

It happened on a Tuesday morning in early October. Mr. Dufour, Max, his sisters, and a few of Marie's intimate acquaintances were all perched on the bed where she lay, with the child in the cradle next to her, when there came a hesitant knock on the door.

Max opened it and found his maid, who whispered:

"If you'd come downstairs right away, sir. Floorke's here and wishes to speak to you—says it's urgent."

Max hurried down the steps. Floorke was in the corridor with his cap on. He doffed it and said in a dull voice, with large, grave eyes, as he panted for air:

"Sir . . . word 'as come that Miss . . . Miss Victoire has died."

"What's that ye say?" Max yelped.

156

"Aye, sir . . . Vreesken came ter tell us . . . not an hour ago . . . ah rushed straight over 'ere on my *vélo*."

"When did it 'appen?"

"This mornin', sir . . . crack of dawn, Vreesken said, between nine an' ten . . ."

Max's face took on a stony expression. His eyebrows were furrowed and his eyes gazed into the distance, at his thoughts.

"Leave yer *vélo* here," he said, "an' wait. Ye'll probably 'ave ter go back 'ome with th'family directly. Go ter th'kitchen for a drop o' beer."

"Very good, sir."

With slow steps, deliberating, Max made his way back upstairs. By the time he opened the door to the room, he had recovered all his self-control. His plan was complete.

"Papa," he said to Mr. Dufour, "two farmers from Baevel urgently wish to speak to you about a question of property lines."

"Goodness!" cried Mr. Dufour, shooting to his feet. "Did they come all this way for that?"

"Yes," Max replied, and with a nod, he coaxed his father out of the room.

"Aunt Victoire is dead!" he said numbly, as soon as they were alone. Then, hurriedly, nervously, "We must go there at once, you understand? Floorke is here; I'll have him ready the carriage."

Mr. Dufour understood perfectly. He was shaken to the core by the unexpected news, but almost more so by the fact that it had happened in their absence. He was ready in no time; Floorke was already harnessing the horse, and Max was expounding to the maid what to say to the ladies upstairs so as not to upset his wife. "We'll be back as soon as we can," he told her. "Meanwhile, the ladies will just have to have their dinner here."

When, after a wild ride, Mr. Dufour and his son arrived at the Aunts' estate, they found Aunt Clemence and Aunt Estelle shedding hot tears, encircled by the Reverend Father, the doctor, and the *notaire* from the village.[1] They heard the story of how it had happened, so suddenly and unexpectedly, just after she had finished a cup of broth and eaten a biscuit. The father and son wore grim expressions and let out pitying cries and then remained there, stony and motionless, as if waiting for something that was about to happen. But

---

1 Translator's note: The *notaire* (Dutch: *notaris*), or civil-law notary, is a university-educated legal professional who works with documents such as contracts and wills. At the time of this story, the village *notaire* was one of the most respected local worthies.

nothing happened. The priest and notary were the first to rise to their feet and say their farewells, as though they had completed their mission there, and the doctor slipped out into the room where the dead woman lay. When he returned, a while later, he whispered to the gentlemen, "Would you like to see her?"

They followed the doctor on tiptoe, accompanied by the two sobbing nurses. They had come as fast as they possibly could, but even so, they had the obscure feeling that they had arrived too late.

They could hear the soft sputter of the candles in the dark room, and they saw the waxy yellow face of the dead woman, in solemn slumber, with her yellow hands folded around a rosary. They kneeled and prayed . . . At the foot of the bed was a nun from the convent, as black and motionless as a statue.

XV.

AUNT VICTOIRE was buried with such pomp as the village had never witnessed before. Only years earlier, when the old baroness in the castle had died, had there ever been anything close to it.

For days on end, the three church bells had sounded their long, solemn death-knells, morning and evening, and on the day of the funeral, four priests carried the body to the gate of the country house.

It was a lovely, quiet morning, with a delicate misty-blue sky and the glittering gold of autumnal tones in the drooping boughs of the trees. The four priests wore magnificent vestments, all white and black velvet and silver, shining in the subtle light like solemn miracles of unmatched splendor, and the silver crosses high on their chests shot white sparks, while the red cassocks of the choirboys were like big, bright flowers swaying in the sun.

The orphans from the Poorhouse, led by the silent black nuns, wore long mourning veils and carried lit wax candles. They wept, very slowly and discretely, with downcast eyes.

Behind the body were Mr. Dufour and Max, in tailcoats and white ties, their heads bare, holding top hats with wide mourning bands. They were followed by the village dignitaries, the Aunts' servants and tenant farmers, and half the local population. Here and there were the waiting carriages that had brought visitors from elsewhere.

Deep within, Max felt the lustrous radiance of the ceremony, which reflected on him and ennobled him. This was how it could and should be. And he was as proud as if it were his own doing, because he had the feeling that as the Aunts' lawful heir, he was helping to pay the high costs of the magnificent funeral. He already knew the terms of the will; he knew that both he and his sisters would receive a not inconsiderable inheritance; but the bulk of the deceased woman's fortune went to the surviving Aunts, and large provisions had also been made for funeral expenses and countless Masses for the dead in the church and in the convent. So the priest and the nuns were also heirs of a kind, not to mention the *notaire* and the doctor, who would submit heavy bills of their own. Even the old kitchen maid Eemlie had been remembered with a tidy sum, and as she had very bad teeth, she had also been left the Aunt's gold-plated dentures. But they did not fit in her mouth; she had decided to sell them.

Max knew and understood all this, and it heightened his sense of self-confident superiority.

In the church, which had been strewn with straw as if for the funeral of a member of the peerage, the catafalque was ringed with candles as thick as arms. The women sat on the left, the men on the right, and the organ and the songs echoed solemnly amid the rising odors of incense, while the four priests officiated in the choir in their full splendor, as noble as saints.

At the start of the offertory, Mr. Dufour removed his overcoat, which he had kept on because of the chilly air in the church, and, holding a wax candle, approached the altar rail, where he gave the gilded communion plate a devout kiss.

Solemn and dignified, with an expression of deep gravity and a sharpened beard, Max followed his father's example, and then came all the other men, the hundreds and hundreds who had traveled from far and wide to that momentous funeral. Mr. Dufour and Max, who had returned to their seats, looked on with intense concentration at all who went forward and gave to the collection plate. Great pride washed over them when

162

they saw the elderly baron and his son pass by, as well as several aristocrats and dignitaries from neighboring towns. Max's cheeks turned the color of fire and he jogged his father's elbow when he saw the Count of Villermont, the president of the Provincial Council, going forward with a candle in his hand. That was a tribute paid to him, to Max, as a member of that council.

After the gentlemen, there came the long procession of farmers and common people. Mr. Dufour and Max recognized many of the Aunts' tenants—gnarled old farmers in their worn and faded best, which they aired only once every so many years, on the most momentous occasions. Then a few more gentlemen went forward, and among them they suddenly, and not without some dismay, recognized Raymond!

"*Est-ce que vous lui avez fait adresser une lettre de faire part?*" Max whispered to his father, in French.

"*Pas le moins du monde!*" Mr. Dufour whispered back.[1]

They followed his every move with narrowed eyes.

He was suitably dressed, in black with gray gloves. It seemed to them he had grown a little

---

1 "Did you have an invitation sent to him?" / "Absolutely not!"

thinner and paler. They couldn't tell whether he glanced toward the ladies' side, because the great mass of the catafalque concealed him for a moment, but when he was in sight again, he glanced at the father and son in passing, in the same natural, ordinary manner that anyone else might. Mr. Dufour pretended not to see him, but Max gave him a cool, stern look and did not return his nod. He disappeared into his seat behind a column.

When the men had finished their offertory, it was the women's turn. They were almost unrecognizable, swathed in thick mourning veils from head to foot. Even so, one could guess that it was Aunt Clemence leading the way, stiff and stern, candle in hand. Aunt Estelle could be recognized by her sorrowful weeping, but it was almost impossible to tell who came next: Clara, Adrienne, or Edmée.

There was one person in the church who knew for certain, however, and that was Raymond.

He had come to the funeral for her alone, for Adrienne, for the chance to take a good, long look at her.

From his chosen seat, hidden from Mr. Dufour and Max by a pillar, he could take her in from afar. She saw him too, and now and then their eyes met.

Raymond seethed with a greater love and passion than he had ever felt before. In the majestic funereal atmosphere of the church where Aunt Victoire was being laid to rest with such overwhelming if faintly absurd grandeur, surrounded by rising incense fumes and the endless reverberation of solemn song and music, he felt only the pressing need to hold her close, to take her in his arms and protect her, to bring her joy in life and rescue her from death. It was as if a thousand voices inside him were crying, "Live! Live! And help her to live, so that she does not meet the same fate as that old woman lying there on the bier, who died without ever knowing what life was!"

His eyes said what he felt with such passion, and it was as if she understood his silent language; a slight blush colored her cheeks, and now and then she pushed the black mourning veil aside as if suffocating under its constriction. Then she would gaze out at him for an instant with eyes of rapture, and her lips would move as if giving him silent, pining kisses. She looked more beautiful than ever to him in those gloomy mourning garments; her blonde hair, her fresh color, the full yet slender forms of her ripening, womanly body, put him under an intoxicating spell that made the contrast with the setting even more agonizing. Yes, life . . . life . . . a life with her! His heart pounded; he had to clench his nervous, shaking hands together, as tightly as he could, to keep himself from rushing to her in a fit of madness and running off with her as if she were his prey!

The solemn priests, bearing crosses and censers, formed a circle around the bier and, their voices resounding with the drone of the organ, sang the final songs. Now, for the first time, Aunt Victoire's soul seemed to separate from her mortal remains for good, and to rise to heaven in the noble odor of incense. Only here, only now, had it come: the end of that life she had never lived, and thus she was carried solemnly away, very slowly and full of belated glory, to the gloomy crypt of oblivion.

The bells clanged in the high tower, the people kneeled with bared heads and then came, one by one, to throw scoops of soil down onto the coffin. There were no flowers, because Aunt had not wanted them; and there were no tears, because she left behind no children who could grieve for her.

Aunt had not lived!

XVI.

THEY had made their decision; it was firm, as firm as a rock . . .

Raymond, a man of action, was unwilling to go on delaying. After what he had experienced at Aunt Victoire's funeral, after the old maid had been sent off into eternity with absurd pomp and abhorrent splendor, after the two surviving Aunts and the rest of the family had basked in the reflected glory, after Mr. Dufour had so conspicuously ignored him, after his old friend Max had glared at him in uncloaked, icy hostility, he knew enough. They would never, of their own accord, permit him to marry Adrienne. Only two paths were left to him: give her up voluntarily, once and for all, or elope with her!

They would elope; the decision was firm. He had made her choose, yes or no, and she had said "yes"!

Yes, yes, yes! With stubborn determination she had said it. She too knew and sensed that there was no other way out.

She was ready. All he had to do was decide the date. For his part, he had made his arrangements. There would be a carriage waiting for them in the evening, at a certain time, off the paved road near the spot by the hedge where they had met before. The only thing he was still waiting for was the absence of the moon, which now rose too early and made the nights too bright.

They each found themselves in a state of nervous, excited agitation. It was tolerable in the daytime, but the nights were unrelenting, unbearable torture. He no longer knew any peace; he could hardly eat; he looked pale and thin; the unhealthy strain made him irritable. "What's up wi' ye; what's made ye stop eatin'?" Manse kept coming to ask him. But the intrusive familiarity of the old kitchen maid, which he was otherwise happy to tolerate, now infuriated him, and with a brusque gesture he would send her away and, quivering with anger, forbid her to poke her nose into his business. Manse was in a terrible state and spent half the time weeping in the kitchen, and Tieldeken trembled when she served him and hurried out of the dining room as fast as she could.

But the nights . . . the nights! Early in the evening, he saw the moon rise in the East, full-bellied and dull orange over the black trees, and he thought to himself, "Only so many more days, and then the night will come, it has to!" He longed for

168

it, he hungered for it, and yet . . . its fateful inevita-
bility, its inescapable quality, its insistent necessity,
sometimes filled him with a kind of horror. What
was he about to do? Run away from everything
dear to him: his house, the life of the farm, his
devoted servants, his faithful animals! It seemed
an impossibility, a monstrosity. Sometimes, when
he saw Manse and Tieldeken doing their work
for him, so faithful and so unsuspecting, or when
Ooh-ooh and Impikoko gazed at him with bright,
questioning eyes, he had to look away so as not
to burst into tears. No, it was impossible, it was
intolerable; he felt he would never have the cruel
courage; and quivering, he sat down at the table to
write to her. But no sooner had he begun his letter
than the pen fell from his hands; the cheerlessness
of what his life would become without her gaped
before him like an abyss. He had to have her; he
could not live without her.

For Adrienne it was different, but torture all the
same. Adrienne no longer struggled; she suffered
. . . She had become defenseless, as it were. She
had no more power of resistance; she let herself
go, ready for anything. She kept herself occupied
with little details. What would she take with her
when she fled, and how would she manage to
gather her things without drawing any attention
or suspicion? For days, she had wandered around
the garden in agitation until she finally found a

spot, under a wood pile, where she concealed a very small traveling bag. There! She was ready! Now he would have to come. She waited . . .

She waited . . . and it was as if all the other life in her had come to a standstill. In her heart, she felt she no longer lived with her family. Her father, her sisters—all strangers to her. She registered their conversations mechanically and did not understand what they were saying. She saw her sisters occupied with their embroidery, as she so often had been, and wondered what it could signify and how a person could fill her hours that way. She would sit idle, with a vacant stare and her hands in her lap, and when Clara and Edmée voiced their surprise, she would start and look at her sisters as if in sudden bewilderment.

Something strange had come into her eyes, a lost, glassy look. Once Clara asked her something and instead of answering, she looked her sister full in the face with a dazed expression and said nothing.

"Oh, Adrienne, what's *wrong* with you?" Clara wailed in distress.

Then Adrienne too became distressed, turning fiery red. "What did you ask me just now?" she said, and when Clara repeated the question, she gave such a peculiar answer that her sisters, baffled, sat motionless for a long while, staring at her in something close to fear.

XVII.

THEN at long last the letter arrived, the final letter, the decisive letter . . . Floorke handed it over to her with exceptional secretiveness, as if he knew its contents.

It was no more than a few lines in a shaky hand:

> The day after tomorrow, at the stroke of seven, the carriage will be in the appointed place. I shall wait for you *in* the garden, by the hedge. We go to meet our happiness, our life!
>
> A thousand kisses,
>
> Raymond

He was ready. By early afternoon he was ready, unable to turn himself to anything else. The Verstratjes had come riding up that morning, but he had hid in his room, too nervous to see them, and ordered Manse to tell them he wasn't in.

Once the Verstratjes were gone, he had spoken to Manse, telling her he'd be going away for a few days and wasn't quite sure when he'd be back—but would let her know in good time. Probably no more than four days, a week at most. Manse had made almost no reply but limped to the kitchen, where she sat in a chair and wept.

It was four o'clock. Three more endless hours to wait! How would he endure it? The red sun was making its slow descent toward the west, but there was still so much day, so much torture ahead. He no longer knew where to go; he could not think how to struggle through those last, torturous hours.

The dogs followed him on foot, as if they sensed that their master was going to leave them. For the hundredth time, he went into the stables and caressingly patted the thighs and the manes of the sorrel and the gray. He spoke to them as if they were human and fed them sugar lumps. And he was just heading for the open door when a shadow fell over the entrance.

"Sir . . . are ye there?" asked a muffled voice, husky and thick with emotion.

The tone made him apprehensive. "Who's there?" he called out nervously.

"'tis me, sir . . . Floorke."

"Floorke! . . . What's amiss? What brings ye here?"

"Oh, sir . . . sir . . . Miss Adrienne!" Floorke said with a sudden sob.

"What is it? What is it?" he yelled.

"Shay's like to 'ave gone mad, sir! Shay's runnin' all abaht th'garden screamin'. Shay willna stop callin' for ye, so they sent me here ter ax ye ter come. They canna do a thing wi'er!"

"Who . . . who sent ye?" he cried, quaking.

"Mester Dufour . . . Mester Max . . . ever'one! Come wi' me, sir. Shay's bin carryin' on ever since th'noonday!"

He ran back to the house like a man possessed. In an instant, he was on his bicycle, racing into the village with Floorke, who had come on his own "*vélo*."

By the time he arrived, darkness was falling. The sun, red as a conflagration, was sinking behind the trees in Mr. Dufour's garden. He saw four people standing by the fence, watching and listening. From the depths of the garden came a sudden sharp scream.

Trembling, he jumped off his bicycle and ran around to the back of the house.

Soon Mr. Dufour came up to him, with Clara and Edmée weeping at his side.

"It's terrible . . . abominable!" Mr. Dufour said in a choked voice. "Do you hear that? Do you hear it? She's calling for you! It's been going on all afternoon. Max, the doctor, and two nuns from the convent are chasing after her, trying to catch her, but they can't. She's gone wild, savage, she'd gouge out their eyes! . . . Come with me . . . Maybe . . . if she sees you, she'll calm down."

As if in a hideous nightmare, Raymond followed. Again, they heard her, shouting his name shrilly in the depths of the garden. They walked straight across the wide lawn to the edge of the shrubbery and came to a halt.

"You see her! You see her! There, in front of the woodpile!" Mr. Dufour whispered.

Raymond, whose eyes were misted, first had to adjust to the surroundings. For a moment, he saw nothing but the tragic red of the setting sun and the stark black outlines of the tree trunks. Then he made out two dark silhouettes—which he had taken at first for two trunks—inching forward. It was the two nuns from the convent, shuffling quietly toward two other dark forms, which Raymond identified as Max and the young village doctor. All four silhouettes looked around, and one, the doctor, crept over to Mr. Dufour and Raymond.

"Do you see her standing there?" the doctor whispered in Raymond's ear. He did not see her; tears clouded his eyes; he was too upset.

"There . . . by that woodpile . . . under those drooping branches," the doctor explained.

All at once he saw her! . . . He saw her standing motionless, dressed in black, with a chalk-white face. And suddenly, he heard the piercing cry again—"Raymond! . . . Raymond! . . ."—stabbing into flesh and bone.

"Perhaps you could step forward and call her over to you . . . gently, very gently . . ." the doctor whispered.

Raymond obeyed, as if in a dream. He shuffled a few steps forward, while the others hid behind the bushes, and he said, in a gentle, tender voice:

"Adrienne . . . Adrienne . . ."

A moment of deathly silence! . . . A silence to make you shudder and shiver. And the very next moment, a kind of wild flapping . . . a figure running, practically flying into his arms . . . an embrace . . . arms and legs clasping tight, almost throwing him off balance.

The others shot over right away. With all their force, they grabbed her and pulled her off him. But she gave such a horrible caterwaul that they soon let go of her.

"No, no, that's not the way, that's not the way!" the panting doctor insisted. "Gentle . . . gentle . . . isn't that right, Adrienne?" he murmured, as if to a child. "Gentle . . . ever so gentle . . . and Raymond will stay with you . . . won't he, Adrienne?"

She settled down at once. Then, throwing her arms around Raymond's neck passionately, she kissed him on the mouth with ravenous sighs, her eyes shut tight.

"Good . . . good . . . you see . . ." said the doctor, gesturing frantically at the others to keep silent. "That's the way . . . just like that . . . and now we'll take a nice little walk to the house, and Raymond will be right here with us . . . yes, that's right . . . he'll stay right beside us . . . he's not going anywhere . . . and soon we'll take a little trip in a carriage . . . and won't it be lovely, just lovely."

They coaxed her into the house, entering through the back door to the kitchen, where the shocked and flustered maids were weeping, and made their way to the little salon where the sisters always sat. She would not let go of his hands for an instant, and now and then she kissed him, long and passionately, with her eyes shut.

"A carriage . . . a carriage . . ." the doctor whispered hurriedly to Max.

Raymond thought of the carriage he had ordered, which must be waiting for them even now. With bitter wistfulness, he beckoned the doctor and whispered a few hasty words in his ear. The doctor rushed off.

A few minutes later he was back and announced in happy relief, "The carriage is outside."

"Come with . . . come with . . . you're coming with!" Adrienne cried, wild-eyed, squeezing Raymond's hands passionately in her own.

"Of course," he said with a gentle smile. "That goes without saying. But first, won't you be a dear and have something to drink? It's a long trip, and you haven't had your supper. You need something fortifying."

He handed her a full glass of what looked like wine, and she drank it without protest. "Tastes good," she said, and she wanted more. "No, not too much," said the doctor, when she asked for another glass.

They rose. In the dim salon, where only a low flame was burning, the nuns helped her dress with a wealth of loving care. Martha, her eyes red with weeping, placed a packed bag in the corner. Clara and Edmée, who could no longer stand to watch, were out in the corridor sobbing. Mr. Dufour and Max were striving to maintain their composure.

As if in a dream, they left the house and went toward the carriage. She did not let go of his hand. He was as white as a sheet and trembled. The doctor followed. In the glow of the carriage lamps, they saw a few coarse, inquisitive faces, which the doctor fixed with a glare of fury and contempt.

They stepped inside, Adrienne and Raymond hand in hand in the back seat, the doctor in the front seat. The driver flicked his horses with his whip, and the carriage went rattling away.

✳

When they had been on the road for more than half an hour, Adrienne's hand released his. She had fallen asleep. The doctor looked at her and whispered, "It worked. She won't wake up until tomorrow morning. I gave her a heavy dose."

"And tomorrow . . . and the day after . . . and all the other days?" Raymond asked, with a catch in his voice.

The doctor shrugged.

"No one can say . . . we must hope . . . hope . . ." he whispered.

Raymond collapsed into himself, as if broken, and long-suppressed tears flooded over his cheeks. Was *this* to be their escape, their magnificent journey to liberation and happiness?! The rattling wheels of the carriage seemed to be rolling over his broken heart.

The carriage arrived in the town, and after making its way down many a silent, deserted street, it stopped in front of a large building in a solitary square. The doctor stepped out and rang the bell.

A nun with a fresh face under her white wimple opened the heavy door.

"We've brought the patient I phoned you about," he said.

The nun nodded with a sweet smile, and right away, a few of her sisters came to help. They went to the carriage and looked inside.

Adrienne was still sprawled back over the cushions, sleeping. They removed her very gently and carried her inside.

Raymond, through his tears, watched as she was carried off like a corpse.

"Wait here for a few moments," the doctor said. "You can't come into the room with me. I have to sort everything out with the assistant."

Raymond shut his eyes and sagged into the cushions.

XVIII.

LIFE is made for the healthy and the strong. They may suffer and grieve for a time, but they rebound.

When, after weeks and months of grief and of being tossed back and forth between hope and hopelessness, Raymond finally knew that Adrienne would not recover, he resigned himself, bit by bit, to the situation. He was again seen on horseback with the Verstratjes, still sad and downcast, yet reviving. What a strange detour his life had taken! How was it possible that he, who had never spared a thought for Adrienne, had fallen for her with such unexpected passion, just because the Verstratjes had told him that *she* was in love with *him*! Was that true love, or was it the weird, unfathomable power of suggestion? Even Raymond could not say. It had been like an illness. He had gone through it and suffered under it, and now came slow recovery and consolation. He felt no guilt. He did not believe he was to blame for anything. A dark destiny had willed it so.

In his heart, he still cherished a deep tenderness toward her. He thought of her often and always with great warmth and love. But he could not help it that he was healthy and normal or that, in him, life triumphed over destruction. He could not help it that the newborn spring was as fresh and delightful as ever, or that the amorous birds sang, or that the mild earth smelled of flowers and life was calling him . . . calling him, with all its energies.

So he revived; and his revival was an irrepressible rejoicing as after a long, severe illness. Never before had he so loved his life and the life of his farm. Never before had he felt so attached to old Manse; never before had he appreciated Tieldeken's faithful service as he did now. And although for a while he had avoided the Verstratjes, they now became his regular companions again. Even the animals—his sorrel, his gray, and Impikoko and Ooh-Ooh, were all friends regained after a period of ungrateful indifference and neglect.

Among the Dufours, however, there was not yet any sign of recovery or revival. Cruel tragedy weighed on them with all its destructive energy. The old gentleman could not get over it; the girls were ashamed and avoided company. The Aunts, Aunt Clemence in particular, put all the blame on Raymond, but the one who felt hardest hit

181

was Max. In June, he had stood for election to Parliament and been defeated. He did not doubt for an instant that the sole cause had been the damage done by Adrienne to his and his family's reputation; and he seethed with hatred and protest against his hapless sister. The others thought of her day and night, awaiting each scrap of chilling news from the doctor, who visited her now and then in the insane asylum; he, Max, wished to hear nothing more of her, and insisted that in his presence her name should never be mentioned again.

Poor Adrienne! . . . The news brought to them now and then by the young village doctor about her condition was anything but comforting or hopeful. At first, she had ranted and raved for months like a savage, leaving them no choice but to put her in a straitjacket; a phase of continuous crying followed; and now her moods varied: occasional terrible rage was followed by fits of deep depression and tears. Mr. Dufour and his daughters always begged permission to visit her; but the doctor advised them against it in the strongest possible terms, not only for their sake—for it would bring them nothing but pain and sorrow—but, above all, for the invalid herself, for whom all emotion and every memory of the past was to be avoided. They would have to be patient and wait.

XIX.

THEY showed patience, and they waited, and at last they were admitted to see the sick woman. Mr. Dufour, who had longed for that day with such dread, decided at the last moment not to join them after all. He feared he could not suppress his emotions; it would be better, he said, for the sisters to pay this first visit on their own. He could go with them later.

Their carriage set off on a quiet, bright September morning. Peace and abundance seemed to fill the clean, pure air. Wherever they looked, there were people in the fields, and high in the blue, larks warbled their dreamy song of love. The sun made the haystacks glitter like golden bells.

They reached the city, and Floorke stopped the carriage in front of the large red brick building in the solitary square. The old-fashioned, white-washed houses with green shutters stood dreaming all around them; a cluster of children were playing marbles in the shade of the chestnut trees, whose foliage was already turning brown.

They rang the bell, and the nun with the friendly smile who had admitted Adrienne came to open the heavy oak door. Clara and Edmée, pale and emotional, saw a long, wide, brightly lit corridor with many little doors, and French windows at the far end. Black nuns with white wimples bustled to and fro; the air was filled with the smell of good food.

They were led into a little room and told to wait there. It was a bare, whitewashed place with no furniture but a table and a few chairs, and a great crucifix instead of a mirror above the mantelpiece. The large building's reverberations came numbly through the walls.

The door opened and a nun entered, her face as fresh as a rose and her beautiful eyes glowing with inner peace and contentment. "I am Soeur Perpétue. I care for your sister," she said with a charming smile. "Would you come with me?"

"How is she doing?" Clara asked, nervously.

"Oh, very well, better and better. She's all settled down now," the nun replied.

"Do you believe, *ma soeur*, that she can still recover?" Clara asked, almost pleading.

In an instant, the nun's expression turned grim.

"God's mercy is great. We must hope and pray," she said fervently. "Will you please come with me?"

They followed her down the corridor. On the left, a double door was wide open, revealing a large ward packed with women.

"Is that it?" asked Clara, trembling.

"Oh, no," said the nun, "this is third class. But let's pop inside for a minute. You can have a look."

After a moment's hesitation, they followed her. No sooner had they entered the large ward than a woman grabbed the nun by the arm and began to chatter away. Soeur Perpétue smiled and spoke calm words to soothe the woman as she brought her to her chair against the white wall.

There sat another woman, motionless, her hands folded in her lap, silently weeping. Her eyes stared out ahead of her and her tears ran steadily down her cheeks without any attempt on her part to dry them. The nun spoke softly to her. The woman gave the nurse a brief glance and slowly shook her head. Her hands did not move, her tears went on flowing.

In the rear of the ward was a long table around which many women sat, all dressed in gray. They were eating lunch, served by nuns. Not a word was spoken. They sat there as if in a dream, each in their own separate life.

"Are all those women mad?" Clara asked in a whisper.

Soeur Perpétue said nothing but nodded her head.

"And they never talk to each other?"

"Almost never. They are perfect strangers to one another. They have no points of contact."

With heavy steps, they left the sinister ward.

"This way," said the nun, going up a flight of stairs.

They followed her, their hearts pounding. They went down a long corridor and stopped at the last door. The nun lowered her head to the keyhole and appeared to be listening. She smiled and nodded. They could go inside. She softly opened the door.

"Adrienne, look who we have here!" she said in a happy, cajoling voice.

Beside the bed, in an armchair, sat a figure in plain gray garments. Two hands were picking away at something; two strange eyes looked up, and a slightly crooked mouth sketched a weak smile. The hands abruptly ceased their picking.

"Adrienne . . . do you recognize me?" Clara asked in a guarded tone.

"Clara . . ." answered a strange voice, somehow distant.

"Do you recognize Edmée too?"

"Edmée . . ." answered the distant voice.

The nun smiled, pleased and contented.

"You see, she recognizes you perfectly well. Don't you, Adrienne?"

Adrienne nodded and gave her sisters a short, sharp look. Then she turned to the nun and said, with worried eyes and a labored voice:

"She slept well, *ma soeur*, but she's not ready for her walk yet."

With a wink to the sisters, the nun leaned over the bed, which held a large, dressed-up doll, as Clara and Edmée now noticed in surprise.

"Yes, she's sleeping. She's still a little tired," the nun said, straightening up. "But you'll see: she'll soon be back on her feet."

"It's so hard sometimes, *ma soeur*," the invalid moaned, as she resumed her picking.

Clara, gripped by a sudden despair, had turned and gone to the window. She could no longer bear to witness the sorrowful scene. She let out muffled sobs, her shoulders heaving. Edmée came to her side and dully pleaded with her to control herself.

The nun made a quick, discreet gesture; perhaps the time had come to leave. They had seen her now; they could return whenever they wished and stay longer.

Clara, fighting back her emotions, went up to Adrienne. She saw threads of silver already running through the bowed blonde head.

"Adrienne, my darling," she said with great tenderness. And she embraced her sister with such love as she had never shown her before. Edmée followed her example.

Adrienne, indifferent, was already picking again. It was for clothes for her child, the nun explained. She had, oh, so much to do; she feared she could never finish in time.

Slowly, their sad eyes on their tragic sister, the girls backed toward the door. They would have been so glad of a single word from her, a single look of recognition; but the nun gave a slow, resigned shake of her head. No, the poor creature would not look up again; she was much too busy picking . . .

The door, which was opened softly and shut still more softly, put her out of sight of her sorrowful sisters.

In the waiting room, to which they returned for a moment at the nun's request, they sat and spoke of Adrienne a while longer. One question burned on Clara's lips; she hardly dared ask it. Yet finally she did, faltering with emotion, her voice trembling and her cheeks burning.

"And . . . and . . . the man, *ma soeur*, with whom she was so infatuated . . . does she ever speak of him?"

"Oh, no, not any longer, never!" the nun said with her most charming smile. "It's as if that passion had never existed." And she calmly explained, "At first it was horrible—it wasn't just him, but any man she happened to see: the doctor, the assistant, the orderlies, no matter who! She would screech like a woman possessed and tear the clothes from her body! It was her illness. She couldn't help it. We've seen it all before!" the nun reassured them.

Their faces red with embarrassment, the two sisters cast down their eyes. Clara was sorry she had asked. She bit her lips, and tears rolled down her cheeks.

"Oh, my dear, don't shed any tears over that," the nun said in her soothing voice. "We look at that with different eyes. We see and hear so many things here!"

"You are a saint!" Clara cried, with a muffled sob. And she gave the nun's hand a passionate squeeze.

"We follow our vocation and perform our duty," was the nun's simple, humble reply. And with a smile of serene peace, she showed the two sisters out.

XX.

WHEN the sisters' returned to Mr. Dufour's house, they found the Aunts waiting there, still in deep mourning, to hear the account of the visit.

Mr. Dufour wept with sorrow, and Aunt Estelle folded and unfolded her hands as if in silent supplication, but Aunt Clemence was grim and implacable. It was not Adrienne, but Raymond, on whose shoulders she laid the blame for everything. To her he was a common criminal, a vile seducer, who had led the poor girl to ruin. And she said terrible things about him, which she claimed to have heard from the most reliable sources: he went out riding every day again with those despicable good-for-nothings the Verstratjes, and she'd heard from people, the best-informed people, that he had turned for consolation to Tieldeken, the cousin of that old kitchen maid of his, a mere child, and already his latest victim on the road to ruin—it was scandalous! One fortunate thing, at least: poor Adrienne had escaped his bestial lusts in time.

The others said little, and Clara sat pondering. Adrienne's misfortune had awoken something in her that she had never felt or suspected before. She too had been angry, even furious, at Raymond, but was no longer. Now she sometimes wondered if he might have been, not the destroyer, but the rescuer of their collective happiness. Hadn't he offered their dead household, from which all joy had been banished, the gifts of love and life! Thanks to him something had blossomed, or tried to blossom; but the Aunts had nipped it in the bud. And she could never forgive the Aunts for that; and her blood boiled when she heard Aunt Clemence shower him with her relentless abuse. She could no longer stand to listen, and the words slipped out:

"Oh, Aunt, so you say, but wouldn't it have been a hundred times better, both for poor Adrienne and for us all, if no objection had been raised to that marriage—if she had gone ahead and married him?"

"Buh . . . buh . . . buh . . ." said the stupefied Mr. Dufour.

"What?! What's that you say?" Aunt Clemence cried, incredulous. "Marry! A villain such as him!"

"He is no villain, Aunt," Clara rebutted with calm determination. "He loved Adrienne with all his heart. He would have made her happy."

Aunt Clemence scrutinized her niece with her sharp eyes, as if all of a sudden she saw a stranger in front of her. Never before had the family experienced anything like it; never before had anyone dared to say no after one of the Aunts had said yes. With a curt gesture, she brushed away the pleading hands of Aunt Estelle, who was trying to come between them and reconcile them, and said, in a hiss:

"So, Clara! You would have approved of that marriage? They would have had your consent?"

"Buh . . . buh . . . buh . . . *du calme . . . du calme* . . ." Mr. Dufour tried to smooth things over. Aunt Estelle had tears in her eyes. Edmée, her eyes fixed on the floor, sat in her chair trembling.

"Yes, Aunt, they would have had my fullest consent," Clara said without hesitating.

"And you blame us, your Aunts, for disapproving of the match and throwing up obstacles?"

"I do."

It was as if another woman spoke through Clara's lips. She herself did not know, did not understand, where she found the courage, but it spoke from within her, calm but determined, like a long-suppressed force of nature that at long last bursts forth and will be held back no longer. Never before had she known such inner peace. She felt the powerful beating of her heart, but it was slow and regular, like something that could maintain perfect self-control. She withstood Aunt Clemence's sharp look, without lowering her eyes for a second, and went on talking, in a voice that was like the voice of a stranger within her, declaring with utter confidence, and without the least anxiety:

"Yes, I deplore what you did—not Aunt Estelle, but you and Aunt Victoire. With all due respect, I would even say your course of action was wrong. You have always lived outside real life—and, I might add, so have we. You see, I am not just accusing you—I am accusing us. We feared you and went along with you out of miserable calculation. We never dared to do anything of which you might have disapproved, because you are wealthy and we are your heirs, because we feared that later you would make us pay. We let time pass; we ruined our lives; we allowed ourselves to shrivel in seclusion, as you yourselves have shriveled, without enjoying the slightest taste of life as it is—true, rich, and real. Now it is too late for us, as it is too late for you; Adrienne's tragedy has taken away our last chance; we shall become Aunts like you, fit only to live for Max's children, just as you were fit only to live for us."

Aunt Clemence had sprung to her feet in savage fury. "For shame!" she howled. "For shame!" as Aunt Estelle and Edmée burst into tears and Mr. Dufour paced back and forth, raising his arms over his head like a lunatic. "For shame! For shame!" she cried out, her eyes bulging. "I do not wish to remain here another instant! I wish . . . I wish . . ." Words failed her; she twisted her head away and collapsed, like a broken thing, into her armchair, crying and sobbing.

Mr. Dufour flew to the door for help. But before he could put his hand on the knob, it seemed to open of its own accord, and there was Max.

"What's the matter? What has happened here?" he barked, as if frozen on the threshold.

"Shut the door . . . shut the door!" Mr. Dufour urged him.

"Open the door!" shrieked Aunt Clemence, flying out of her seat like a harpy. "Open the door! Come, Estelle! We shall never set foot in this house again!" She literally dragged her sister along behind her; they vanished, as if in a cyclone, and a moment later the dumbstruck family saw Vreesken rattling away in the old barouche.

"What on earth has happened here? What's the matter?" Max insisted, as pale as a ghost and shaking with alarm, still nailed to the threshold.

"I have told her the truth," was Clara's blunt answer, as her cold eyes looked her brother up and down.

"The truth . . . What truth?" he said with a shiver.

Mr. Dufour ran out of the room and shut the door behind him with a bang.

"About her attitude toward Adrienne," Clara snapped.

He did not understand; he stood trembling.

"Surely you haven't . . . contradicted her!" he barked hoarsely, now suspecting . . . now seeing all.

She told him, in a few brief, bitter, caustic words.

He leapt toward her, his fists balled as if to strike her.

"What? You wouldn't dare!" she cried, meeting his eyes without fear.

"You have ruined us! My children, ruined. They will disinherit us! You bitch! You bitch!" he bellowed, beside himself.

She looked at him, as cold as ice, unmoved, her eyes full of scorn. She had never had much patience with his petty tyranny; her stubborn nature had always clashed with his; now she hated and despised him.

"You have nothing to fear," she said, mocking him. "They will disinherit me, but not you. On the contrary, you stand to gain; you will receive *my* share as well!"

He gazed at her as if at a madwoman. He snorted like a hippopotamus; his eyes blazed.

"And don't lose your temper with me, because one day I too shall be a wealthy aunt," she went on in wry self-mockery. "Yes, I too, and Adrienne, and Edmée—we too are Aunts . . . Aunts . . . who will never marry, any more than the others will, and one day your children will be our heirs, *if* you do not offend us, *if* you are not ill-mannered and rude to us, as you have been today."

He looked at her, staring, smoothing his beard to a point, his lips pursed tight shut, like a predator eyeing its prey. He said nothing more, nothing, not a single word. He took a deep breath through his trembling nostrils and turned around.

Without a sound, without a gesture, he went to the door, opened it, and left.

In the corridor, his father was pacing back and forth with a frown.

"Where are you off to?" he asked his son.

"To see the Aunts," Max replied.

Mr. Dufour went back into the room.

Each sunk into an armchair, Clara and Edmée were sitting in the rich twilight that gleamed through the windows, with handkerchiefs pressed to their faces, sobbing and weeping.

THE END.

A PARTIAL LIST OF SNUGGLY BOOKS

www.ingramcontent.com/pod-product-compliance
Lightning Source LLC
Chambersburg PA
CBHW050136110726